'I'm assuming that meeting again like this is as much of a surprise to you as it is to me.'

'It most certainly is.' Annabel was delighted Drew had given her the chance to clear that up. 'I had absolutely no idea you were back until I started work here.'

'Supposing you had known?'

What was he driving at? Impossible to tell from that bland expression. 'What difference would it have made? It would have been rather silly, don't you think, to turn down the best job I could get in Inverdon, just because you and I once thought we liked each other rather better than we actually did?'

Drusilla Douglas is a physiotherapist who has written numerous short stories—mainly for Scottish based magazines. Now the luxury of working part-time has provided her with the leisure necessary to embark on novels.

Previous Titles

THE TROUBLE WITH DOCTORS
THE VALLERSAY CURE
SURGEON IN THE HIGHLANDS

A SERIOUS CASE OF CONFUSION

BY

DRUSILLA DOUGLAS

MILLS & BOON LIMITED
ETON HOUSE   18–24 PARADISE ROAD
RICHMOND   SURREY   TW9 1SR

*First published in Great Britain 1990
by Mills & Boon Limited*

© Drusilla Douglas 1990

*Australian copyright 1990
Philippine copyright 1990
This edition 1990*

ISBN 0 263 77026 5

*Set in 10 on 11½ pt Linotron Baskerville
03-9010-51939
Typeset in Great Britain by Centracet, Cambridge
Made and printed in Great Britain*

CHAPTER ONE

ON HER very first day at Inverdon Royal Infirmary, Annabel Kerr discovered that Drew Maitland was back. No matter. She was no longer a green and gullible eighteen-year-old. It took more than a dose of boyish charm and a good profile to unsettle her now. Besides, he was probably married, though just in case he wasn't Annabel took care to keep out of his way. No sense in having him wonder if she had returned on his account— because he might. Drew Maitland had never been short on confidence.

Then, after almost a month of successful evasion, the physiotherapist on Surgical Neurology collapsed in the middle of a gym class and was rushed off to Theatre with an acute appendix. Naturally this was the sole topic of conversation over after-lunch coffee in the physio staff-room, and the receptionist had to shriek to make herself heard above the excited exchanges. 'Miss Tannoch would like to see you in her office, please, Miss Kerr,' she fluted into the temporary calm. 'It's about poor Mrs Craig,' she added as Annabel followed her out.

Annabel had already guessed that—and that Miss Tannoch was going to ask her to take over. Very soon now, she and Drew Maitland would be face to face for the first time in eight years.

'But only if you really don't mind, Annabel,' added the superintendent anxiously, after making her request. The rank and file physios had soon decided that a girl like Annabel with such large and dancing brown eyes

5

must be 'All Right', but Miss Tannoch was still very much in awe of her new deputy. After all, it wasn't every day that lecturers from famous London training schools went back into clinical work. Thirty years at the Royal, and never once on a refresher course, Miss Tannoch was also feeling rather threatened.

Annabel knew this perfectly well and she answered soothingly, 'I'm quite prepared to work wherever I'm needed most, and, as you say, I'm the only other physio with enough of the right experience. Besides, you're the boss, Miss Tannoch,' she added diplomatically.

'Yes, I am, am I not, dear?' acknowledged the boss with an endearing mixture of complacency and relief. 'Now that's settled, I'll arrange to re-allocate your outpatients and then you can get over to DSN right away.'

'Thank you, Miss Tannoch.'

The day she began work here at the Royal Infirmary, Annabel had been taken on a lightning tour of the whole establishment, so she already knew that the Department of Surgical Neurology was quite self-contained—a hospital within a hospital—but the senior sister had been off duty that day and, having her priorities right, Annabel went straight to her office to introduce herself. A cheerful voice called out, 'Come in,' in answer to her knock.

Annabel opened the door and stared, a slow smile breaking over her face. 'Jean Clarke! I don't believe it.'

Once over her own astonishment, the merry-eyed blonde behind the desk was looking just as pleased. 'Jean Fyvie, if you don't mind, young Annabel. I got married four years back.'

'Belated congratulations, then,' offered Annabel.

'Thanks. I kept it in the family, so to speak. Bob is Senior Registrar on Orthopaedics at the General.' Jean looked Annabel over again. 'So the brainy Miss Kerr Barbara Craig told us about is also young harum-scarum Annabel Kerr of the Lower Fourth at Inverdon High! Remember the time I had to give you detention for missing gym?'

Annabel chuckled. 'Will I ever forget? Punishment from the popular head girl was far more wounding than having it dished out by a mere teacher. I'm to be Barbara's locum, by the way.'

'I'd guessed that.' Jean paused. 'But whatever brought you home, when by all accounts you were doing so well in the south?'

'Family problems,' was all Annabel had time to say before the door opened and Drew Maitland appeared in the doorway.

Annabel saw him before he noticed her. His boy's face had settled into firmer lines of maturity; otherwise the lack of change was remarkable—the same suggestion of fitness and strength in his tall, lithe figure, the same plentiful curling dark hair, the same hint of humour lurking in deep-set grey eyes as he greeted Jean. But as they lit on Annabel, humour gave way to a blank, still stare. When Jean introduced them, Drew said matter-of-factly, 'Thanks, Sister, but Miss Kerr and I have met before.'

'Really?' exclaimed Jean, giving Annabel a reproachful look.

'Yes, really,' repeated Annabel, 'but it was so long ago that I'm flattered Mr Maitland remembers. ' She returned his level gaze. 'Apparently congratulations are in order.'

Straight dark brows came together in a frown. 'On the accuracy of my memory?'

'On your consultancy. I'm always happy to hear of an old acquaintance achieving all he set out to do.' Just

a very little dart—and surely she could be forgiven for
it? Heaven knew he'd laid enough emphasis on his goal
when insisting how crazy it would be to make any sort
of commitment right at the beginning of their careers.

Drew smiled thinly. 'How thoughtful—but how do
you know that I have?'

Said for Jean's benefit, thought Annabel, reluctantly
admiring his presence of mind.

After a slightly awkward pause, Drew asked
brusquely, 'Are you merely visiting, or are you taking
over from our unfortunate colleague?'

'I'm taking over.'

'Then you'll need briefing.' He looked at his watch
and then at Jean. 'I'm seeing Seonaid McLeod's parents
at two-fifteen,' he told her in a gentler voice, 'so there's
just about time to show Miss Kerr her patients before
that.' He turned a stolid gaze on Annabel. 'Come along,
then. We'll start with the head injuries.'

He stood aside for Annabel to precede him out of the
office and then led the way in silence to a small but
beautifully equipped ward with six cubicles. Three of
them were occupied. A nurse was adjusting the drip-
feed of one patient, while a young doctor had just taken
a blood sample from another.

'Dr Simpson, House Officer. Miss Kerr, Assistant
Superintendent Physiotherapist, who is standing in for
Barbara,' said Drew. He gave them no time to do more
than nod at one another before continuing briskly,
'You'll have noticed that this is a mixed sex ward, Miss
Kerr. Later, when our patients become aware and
require less intensive supervision, we transfer them to
the appropriate ward.' He came to a halt at the foot of
the third patient's bed. 'Colin Montrose is a thirty-four-
year-old scaffolder who fell twenty feet at his work ten
days ago. On to soft ground fortunately, or he would

probably have sustained more than a moderate concussion/contusion injury.'

'Plus a couple of fractures,' assumed Annabel, noting the plaster casts on right forearm and lower leg.

'Correct, but according to the orthopods they're both quite straightforward,' returned Drew, taking a pencil-slim torch from his top pocket. Gently he lifted each of Colin Montrose's eyelids in turn and shone the light into his eyes. 'Beginning to accommodate,' he murmured with satisfaction. 'You'll be fully with us in a few more days, will you not, old lad?'

Nobody had yet established positively whether or not unconscious patients could hear, so Annabel was glad to note that Drew belonged to the school which believed in talking to them. 'What about his muscle tone?' she asked practically.

'Inevitably there's some increase, but Barbara always insisted that she could get a full range of passive movement fairly easily.' Drew bent over the patient again. 'We'll soon have you out walking over the hills again, Colin,' he promised before moving on to the next bed.

He's also taken the trouble to find out the man's special interests, noted Annabel. But then, whatever his personal shortcomings, Drew Maitland was always an excellent doctor.

'Rather more of an uphill task here, I'm afraid,' he observed soberly as they approached the next patient. 'This is Donnie Helm, who came off his motor-bike six weeks ago and is still not responding. He's also had a severe chest infection, but that's slowly resolving.'

'I thought I recognised the signs. But his head injury—was he not wearing a crash helmet?'

'Yes, or he'd not have survived, judging by the accounts of various witnesses. Apparently he catapulted through the air and landed head first on a concrete traffic island. As it was, there was a fair amount of subdural haemorrhaging—hence the burr holes to clear it away.' Drew looked thoughtfully down at the patient again. 'He's young, so if he comes out of coma fairly soon he should do all right eventually. Providing that he gets the necessary accurate and intensive physiotherapy.'

The eighteen-year-old Annabel who had adored him would have risen to that sort of provocation with much blushing and protesting. This one merely raised a delicately arched eyebrow and remarked quietly, 'I do hope you're not in any serious doubt about that, Mr Maitland.'

'With one of your seniority on the job, I simply wouldn't dare,' he returned imperturbably. 'Where did you do your neurology, by the way?'

'Glasgow initially—where I trained,' she added, because he might not remember that. 'Then I was two years on Professor Landau's unit at the National Institute in London before I went into teaching at St Crispin's.'

'How impressive,' Drew allowed drily as they moved on to the last patient. 'This is wee Seonaid McLeod, who was hit by a car on a pedestrian crossing three weeks ago.' His voice hardened. 'And if I could lay my hands on that driver——' He broke off. 'Anyway, she's coming to now and is at the restless stage, as you can see by the state of her bed.' He soothed the child and replaced her covers before continuing, 'If she goes on like this, we should be able to remove her tracheostomy tube before the end of the week.'

'That's if Seonaid doesn't remove it first,' put in Dr Simpson who, having completed his blood-taking, was following them round. 'She's been fiddling with it quite a lot today. Would it be irritating her, sir?'

'I expect so. That's a common problem with patients emerging from coma. After all, it must be quite mystifying to have such a thing sticking in one's throat.' Drew bent down to check. 'It's quite secure; she'll not manage to dislodge it.' Gently he stroked the child's forehead. 'I know your throat hurts, Seonaid, but it'll soon be better.'

'But why can the tube not come out now, sir?' asked the houseman as they left the ward. 'Her chest seems clear enough.'

'Because, until she's rather more conscious than she is now, there's always the possibility of relapse,' returned Drew patiently, but still raising a faint flush on Dr Simpson's youthful face.

'Why do housemen always ask such elementary questions?' wondered Drew in a tone of resignation as the young doctor left them.

'Because to them the questions are not elementary. We all have to learn,' returned Annabel quietly, 'so it's not a bad idea to remember how it feels to be just starting out.'

Drew took a sharp breath in and frowned at her as if he suspected her answer of having some deeper significance.

She hadn't been getting at him at all, but now she saw that it might have appeared so. 'Sorry about that,' she offered in a conciliatory tone. 'That was the teacher in me speaking. It's taking me longer than I expected to get used to being just a working physio again.'

'I see,' returned Drew with a slight shrug as he opened the door of a two-bedded room. One young woman, her head bandaged, lay either unconscious or sleeping, while another, who seemed to be paralysed down her left side, sat reading in a well-padded arm-chair by the window. 'If I told you they were sisters, would you care to suggest a diagnosis?' asked Drew.

Annabel looked again at the girls and totted up the clues. Not such a difficult problem after all. 'Congenital aneurysm,' she offered confidently.

'Spot on!' approved Drew, with more enthusiasm than he had shown so far. 'The eldest had a subarach-noid bleed two weeks ago after a short history of headaches. Hence the hemiplegia. Having pin-pointed the cause, and recalling the familial incidence, we naturally scanned her brother and sisters. Only the youngest girl showed an arterial bulge, and we tied that off on Saturday.' Having examined both patients, he continued, 'It'll be Claire by the window who needs most of your time. Christine shouldn't need much physio—unless I made some fearful mistake in theatre,' he added, half to himself, when they regained the corridor.

'But you don't make mistakes, if I remember cor-rectly,' observed Annabel frankly.

Drew gave her a sideways considering look. 'I'd say that rather depends on the context,' he returned heavily.

Had his climb to the top not been quite trouble-free, then, or had something gone wrong with his personal life? 'But now I should like to hear your views on stereotaxis in Parkinsonism,' he was saying.

'That's rather a tall order!' protested Annabel, to give herself time to think. 'However, since you ask, it's my experience that it's invaluable for those very rigid patients who don't respond to drug therapy.'

'Mine too—though I would also include those with severe tremor. Can you cope with them post-operatively?'

'Certainly.' What a nerve!

'I'm glad to hear that, as I'll have three for you after Wednesday; that's our main ops day.'

'Fine—I like a bit of variety,' returned Annabel woodenly.

'Don't we all? So now for something completely different. A selection of post-op backs,' he revealed, leading her into another ward. 'All male at the moment, and all prolapsed intervertebral discs.' Swiftly he conducted Annabel round, listing all the variations in history and progress with admirable clarity. Coming out again, he asked, 'In what sequence do you reintroduce spinal movements after operation?'

'Extension, flexion, side-flexion and lastly rotation.' Didn't everybody?

Having noticed the mild surprise in her voice, he said, 'Just checking. Last night, I read a paper in which some guy with an unpronounceable name advocated what he called normal functional movement from day one, post-op.'

'Really? I know ideas are forever changing, but that seems rather extreme. Not to worry, though—it certainly wasn't anybody I've been working with.'

'I'm very relieved to hear it.' Drew allowed himself a fleeting smile. 'I've yet to meet the patient who would be willing to bend down and tie his shoelaces the day after operation.'

'Or able,' supplemented Annabel, smiling back. No awkwardness at all now. But then why would there be? Eight years was a gey long time, and nothing was as dead as a dead love.

While Annabel had been thinking such philosophical thoughts, Drew had been peering through the observation window of a single room. 'Where's Mrs Plockton?' he demanded of a passing nurse, who explained that the patient in question was being helped to have a bath.

'Thank you, Nurse. You'll like Mrs Plockton,' he told Annabel. 'She's remained wonderfully cheerful, despite surgery to remove a cerebellar tumour, and she manages to turn all the inevitable clumsiness into a joke. She needs watching, though, having no idea just how very unsteady she is. Barbara has been treating her in front of a large mirror, so that the patient can monitor her own performance visually.'

'Just what I would have expected,' returned Annabel firmly. Had he really thought she wouldn't know the value of that?

On to yet another ward, which Drew said contained the last of her in-patients. Old Mr Cairns and young Danny McMahon had both sustained head injuries of some severity several months previously. And both were now experiencing residual problems of balance, stiffness, clumsiness and understanding. 'I get the picture, and I'm sure I shall cope,' said Annabel before Drew felt the need to tell her what techniques Barbara had been employing.

'Just as well,' he returned smoothly after a swift glance at the ward clock. 'I've given you all the time I can spare just now, but if there's anything with which I can help while you're working on this unit, please feel free to ask,' he added magnanimously before striding away.

Please feel free to ask. Now why had he thought it necessary to say that, when exchanges of views and information were an integral part of the job? Would he actually prefer her to ask others? Yet he had taken the trouble to show her round himself. Perhaps that was because the only other doctor available that afternoon was the newly qualified Dr Simpson. Annabel shrugged.

Enough of this; if she was going to analyse all her encounters with Drew so minutely, then she'd never get any work done!

Despite her comprehensive introduction, treating every patient for the first time meant very slow progress, and Annabel wasn't at all surprised to find that all the other physios had gone home by the time she returned to the department. It was her turn for evening duty and the staff-room notice-board was dotted with request slips. She arranged them in what seemed to be the right order of priority. Then, as there wasn't time to go home before the evening round—her home village of Durless lay seven miles inland—Annabel changed out of uniform, told the switchboard operator where to find her if she was needed sooner, and crossed the road for an early supper at the wine bar opposite the hospital.

Having given her order, she opened her newspaper at the crossword page, but inevitably her thoughts returned to Drew as she waited for her quiche and salad.

Between leaving school and starting her physio training, she had worked for three months as a nursing orderly at the Royal. She had been assigned to a surgical ward, where the junior houseman—qualified exactly one week and positively bursting with ambition and dedication—was a handsome young Shetlander called Andrew Maitland. He was very nice to all the nurses, but it was Annabel he soon singled out as companion for his limited off-duty time. Reared in an all-female household and fresh from an all-girls' school, Annabel had no experience and no comparisons to make. She promptly fell headlong and completely in love.

Drew fell in love too, but, unlike Annabel, he kept one foot firmly on the ground. And that was how she discovered that mutual love didn't automatically guarantee happy ever after. In a nutshell, Drew had his way to make and he meant to make it unhindered. But that didn't mean they couldn't go on seeing each other, he had insisted. Just that there must be no strings and no promises as yet.

For Annabel—eighteen, innocent and as green as new spring grass—half measures were out. If a man said he loved you, surely he wanted to marry you. And if he didn't, then he couldn't be truly in love. So she went away to college, tore up Drew's letters unread and threw herself into her studies, thereby laying the foundations of a career that people who ought to know had been kind enough to call brilliant.

She hadn't followed Drew's career and hadn't dreamed he might be back at Inverdon Royal Infirmary, with his ambition already achieved. Not that knowing would have made any difference. She'd still have applied for this job, which was the best currently available in the city.

Annabel's supper was brought by the friendly waitress who had often attended to her on previous visits. 'Sorry to keep you waiting, quine,' she apologised, 'but we're short-staffed the night. Wilma's man is on his fortnight off from the oil-rig and they're away to Majorca.'

Annabel smiled back. 'Not to worry, Sharon. I'm not needed over the way for the next hour or so.'

'Not finished yet, then? And you'll have been on your feet all day too—like me. My, but you folk do grand work! I remember when my dad had his operation. . .' Sharon was all set for some reminiscing until summoned back to the present by an imperious snapping of the proprietor's fingers. But before she obeyed, she bent down to whisper, 'I see yon Maitland the surgeon's in again. Anybody'd think he'd got no home to go to!'

Annabel was surprised. She'd had no idea that Drew

ever came here, but, sure enough, when Sharon moved she saw him looking round for a table.

Annabel returned to her crossword and her supper. Then, two clues and several forkfuls later, she sensed somebody beside her. 'Do you mind,' asked Drew, 'but this seems to be the only non-smoking table with a free seat?'

That wasn't just a ploy; a quick glance round confirmed it. 'Of course not. . .' Annabel waved a casual hand at the empty bench opposite.

Drew sat down and then asked conventionally how she had got on that afternoon.

'Quite well, I think.'

'No problems?'

'None—thanks to your excellent briefing.' It was good to find there'd be no difficulty about treating him with the detached friendliness she would adopt towards any male colleague.

'Or more probably to your own expertise,' he returned as easily.

'You're very kind,' considered Annabel with a little smile as she returned to her meal.

'Not entirely,' he persisted. 'I've been glancing through your book on rehabilitation after head injury. It's a brilliant piece of work.'

'Well, thank you,' she returned with a full-scale smile this time. 'I'm hoping it will earn me my Fellowship.'

'Which will be wasted in your present post.' His grey eyes narrowed thoughtfully. 'So why did you take it?'

Sharon came back with Drew's supper at that point, and her face was a picture of lively interest. When she had gone Annabel began, 'It was Hobson's choice really. My elder sister suddenly got married and went to live abroad, which left Mother coping alone with our grandmother. Gran always was a holy terror, but now that she's beginning to dement. . .' Annabel shrugged expressively. 'So I felt I simply must come home and share the burden—at least until we can decide what's to be done.'

'But that's appalling!' Did he mean her mother's predicament, her grandmother's condition, or her own interrupted career? 'Has she been seen by a psychiatrist?'

The second, it seemed. But then Drew and Gran had been the greatest of friends until the break-up. Annabel considered his question. 'Oh, yes, but she happened to be having a good day, and he told my mother she was actually in great shape for seventy-four. So she is—physically. Anyway, we manage.'

There was silence for a bit while they ate and then Drew pushed aside his plate and, leaning forward, said thoughtfully, 'I'm assuming that meeting again like this is as much of a surprise to you as it is to me.'

'It most certainly is.' Annabel was delighted he'd given her the chance to clear that up. 'I had absolutely no idea you were back until I started work here.'

'Supposing you had known?'

What was he driving at? Impossible to tell from that bland expression. 'What difference would it have made? It would have been rather silly, don't you think, to turn down the best job I could get in Inverdon, just because you and I once thought we liked each other rather better than we actually did?' Annabel was very pleased with that. It had come out so casually, and put the whole thing into its proper perspective.

Drew let out his breath on a long sigh and sat back in his seat. 'If that's how you feel, then there would seem to be no reason why we shouldn't work amicably together.'

'I certainly can't see why not.'

'Then how about a glass of wine to seal the bargain?'

Bargain? What bargain? 'Normally I'd accept with pleasure, but this evening I have to go back to work. Very soon,' she added as she picked up her knife and fork again to signify that chat time was over.

Drew kept pace with her, and when Sharon brought their bills he picked up Annabel's with his own.

'Now I really cannot allow——' she began in the tone that was so effective with erring students. It cut no ice with Drew. He just ignored her protest. Nothing for it, then, but to thank him gracefully and resolve to be quicker off the mark next time, should there ever be one.

It was a surprise to discover, on leaving the wine bar, that Drew was also returning to the hospital. 'Are you on call, then?' asked Annabel.

'No. I'm setting up a research programme, so I often work in my consulting-room at nights. It's so damned noisy at home.'

Was it now? She wondered why, and also why a man of his resourcefulness didn't do something about it. But Drew Maitland's private life was not her concern. 'What a good idea,' she applauded instead. 'Then you can always be sure you've got all your material to hand; not to mention a computer, I suspect.'

'There speaks one who knows what it's all about!' Drew regarded her speculatively before saying, 'I'm afraid Barbara's absence is going to set us back somewhat. She was to have been a necessary member of our team.'

Not on your life, Drew Maitland! thought Annabel. There may not be any uncomfortable undercurrents, but I'm not looking for any unnecessary contact. 'I'd offer to help, but I've absolutely no free time, what with looking up old friends and making new ones,' she forestalled him. But why had she been at such pains to paint a picture of a hectic social life?

'Not to mention helping out with Gran—the prime reason for your return,' he supplemented slyly. 'Of course Barbara also has a husband and a house to run, but there——' He broke off deliberately, having successfully implied that Annabel's outside responsibilities were less than Barbara's. 'Well, I mustn't keep you from your patients any longer.'

'Thanks—I've got quite three hours' work, I should think. I shall be visiting the head injuries again, of course.'

'Naturally.'

'Goodnight, then.'

'Goodnight.' Quick as she was, she only just managed to turn away before he did.

While coping with the work, Annabel dismissed that meeting with Drew completely from her mind. There was much less to do than she had expected, as half the patients only required a check visit, rather than the full-scale treatment to clear congested lungs. Eager young physios keen to impress the new deputy boss with their dedication, guessed Annabel indulgently. This meant that she was on the road for home sooner than anticipated.

Soon realising that her mind was less on her driving than on the day's events, she pulled into a handy layby on the outskirts of the city to sort out her thoughts. She got out of the car and leaned on a low stone wall. Below her lay Inverdon, its serried rows of grey stone buildings sparkling in the late evening sun. Wide straight streets, occasional splashes of green park and woodlands and in the distance, between the city and the shimmering blue steel of the North Sea, was the harbour full of fishing boats, their masts appearing no bigger than knitting needles from here. At the very heart of the city was the graceful jumble of the ancient University, with the Victorian Gothic pile of the Royal Infirmary alongside.

When Annabel left, she had glimpsed Drew through the window of his consulting-room, which looked out on to the car park. Drew—so successfully avoided until today. What was that clever phrase she had dreamed up? Thought we liked each other rather better than we actually did. For him, that was undoubtedly true. Unfortunately, not so for her; why else had she never dared to fall in love again—always backing off whenever she felt herself to be in danger? When Drew Maitland rejected her, he had destroyed her faith in her ability ever to hold any man.

How relieved he had been by her light dismissal of their young love. It occurred to Annabel now that the whole purpose of that conversation in the wine bar had been to establish that she'd not been carrying a torch for him all these years; therefore she wouldn't turn out to be a present-day embarrassment. He needn't worry. The emotion had died long ago, even though the scars remained. And now there was Adam; diffident and awkward in his courting, but honest and sincere. Annabel got back in her car and continued along the winding, tree-lined road to Durless.

So far, the little community had escaped the sprawls of modern commuter housing which encircled so many others within easy reach of the city. Everybody in Durless still knew everybody else, and Gran's house was still called Dr Anderson's by those old enough to remember her husband. The sturdy four-square villa had been home to Annabel ever since her father had deserted them more than twenty years before, obliging Mrs Kerr to return home with her two bewildered little

girls. Like its owner, Rowan House dominated the wide
main street from its position next to the kirk.

All askew and half on the pavement stood the ancient
Ford belonging to Gran's lifelong friend Agnes Keith,
who never failed to come round for supper and all the
latest scandal on Mondays. The two friends were going
deaf, though neither seemed to realise that, and Annabel
could hear their voices raised in lively dispute even
before she got her key in the lock.

But tonight they were not alone in Gran's front
sitting-room with the wide bay window, from which she
monitored all the town's comings and goings. A tall,
patient-looking man of about thirty-five laid aside the
Farmer's Weekly and got up from his chair by the fire as
Annabel entered. 'Adam—what a lovely surprise!' she
said warmly, going up to him with hand outstretched.

He swamped it with both his own, but before he could
say anything, Gran cut in with, 'And what time d'ye
call this, miss? There'll be no homework done in this
house again tonight!'

Oh, God, she was having one of her bad days.
Annabel swallowed her dismay and said placatingly,
'I'm very sorry, Gran, but I was—I was kept in.'

'Were you now? Well, I don't doubt you deserved it.'
They never knew whether or not to play along with her
confusion because it came and went so quickly, but
obviously Annabel had made the right choice this time.
'Now you are here, you can just go out to the kitchen
and make us all a nice cup of tea. Take young Adam
with you and give him a chocolate biscuit: he's been
very good and quiet this evening. And say good evening
to his mother.'

'Yes, Gran. Good evening, Mrs Keith. Coming,
Adam?'

Out in the hall with the heavy pine door safely shut,

Annabel murmured, 'She's really muddled tonight, is she not? You must have had a trying time.'

'Not at all. I only got here about an hour ago and she was fine until you came in.' He winced and looked quite distressed. 'I say—look here, Annabel, I didn't mean——'

'Of course you didn't—I know that. The confusion comes and goes for no reason that anybody can see.' She led the way to the big old-fashioned kitchen that Gran would not allow to be modernised. Warming the teapot from the kettle steaming away on the Aga, she added, 'She's getting gey short-tempered as well.'

'And what's new about that?' asked Adam with a rare flash of humour. Adam Keith was by nature serious and earnest. Annabel's mother said it came of being the only child of elderly parents. Agnes had been well into her forties before Adam put in his tardy appearance.

Annabel giggled. 'Good point,' she agreed. 'All the same, it is more marked lately.'

'Perhaps it only seems so to you because you've always been away so much.' He swallowed. 'Annabel, I'm so glad you've come home.'

'So am I. Well, most of the time anyway,' she added, as the remembrance of Drew Maitland came unbidden. She checked the tea-tray to make sure that nothing was missing. Confused or lucid, Gran would be sure to notice.

'I'll take that,' said Adam, though he didn't lift it until he had shyly reminded Annabel that they were going to a concert in Inverdon on Wednesday evening.

'Don't worry—I'd not forgotten. I'm looking forward to it too much,' she reassured him, to be reassured herself by the patent happiness in his eyes. Dear Adam! So kind and dependable. There'd be no risk of heartbreak in believing *him* if he said he loved her!

Far from examining the tea-tray for omissions, Gran
had quite forgotten ordering it. Instead, she wanted to
know what in the world Annabel was thinking of. Didn't
she know that tea at night kept a body from sleeping?

Annabel put on a bright smile and her special manner
for dealing with difficult patients, only to discover yet
again that it didn't work with your nearest and dearest.
It was a great relief when her mother came home and
Agnes reminded her son that he'd need to be up gey
early if he was going to Forfar market next day.

The Keiths away and Gran safely tucked up in bed,
Mrs Kerr and her younger daughter lingered on the
landing for a few words together. 'How was work today?'
Mrs Kerr began.

'I've been given a ward unit to look after.' Annabel
then told the story of poor Barbara's dramatic collapse.

'The poor lassie!' Mrs Kerr was quite a time exclaim-
ing over that before asking, 'And how will you like
working in the wards instead of with outpatients, dear?'

'It'll be a challenge.' Yes, indeed it would—working
with the new Drew Maitland who was so much more
serious and exacting than the one she remembered.

'But no problems, I hope.'

'None that I'll not be able to handle.'

'I'm so glad, dearest. I'd never have asked, you know,
but I'm so very, very glad that you did come home.'

'Then so am I,' affirmed Annabel, planting a kiss on
her mother's soft cheek. But somewhere at the back of
her mind, a tiny seed of doubt was growing.

CHAPTER TWO

AFTER the usual exchange of greetings first thing next morning, Jean Fyvie said, 'You've got an ardent admirer on this unit, Annabel.'

The tiny thrill Annabel felt at that was quite absurd, but her verbal response was just right. 'Oh, goody,' she said. 'Just what I've always wanted.'

'You can scoff,' returned Jean, 'but the poor child is really smitten, after the way he says you stood up for him yesterday afternoon when he made such a ninny of himself over Seonaid's trache tube. He's terrified of Drew Maitland.'

The houseman, then, who must have overheard that exchange as he walked away! 'Oh, it was nothing. Anyway, Dr Simpson only asked the sort of question any of us might in the beginning. But you said "terrified". Why would that be, Jean?'

'Drew Maitland is brilliant, but he drives himself much too hard and he expects equal dedication from all his colleagues. Everybody is afraid of not measuring up—except me, that is.' Jean laughed at the very idea. 'Anyway, just thought I'd better warn you, though from what Barbara has said I gather that you would run Drew a close second in the efficiency stakes.' She became briskly businesslike. 'But you're not here for a rundown on the staff, are you? It's the patients you want to know about. There were no overnight changes. Colin Montrose's conscious level continues to rise slowly and Christine Walker—that's the younger sister on whom Drew operated last Saturday—is fully conscious and quite satisfactory. Peter McEachern, second on the right in the post-op back ward, has been having quite a lot of pain, though, and I'm not too happy about his wound, so a little backpedalling on the exercises might be wise until one of the consultants has pronounced. Otherwise, you're as you were.'

'Thanks, Jean. I'll get started, then.'

'You do that, and if you happen to find yourself with a minute or two to spare around eleven, you'll likely find coffee on the go in here—if I'm not too busy myself. That'd be much quicker for you than going back to Physio for your break.'

'Coffee with the head girl? I say, what a treat for a fourth-former!'

Jean lifted a paperweight. 'Watch it, infant, or you could find yourself on the receiving end of this,' she threatened with a grin as Annabel retreated in pretended fright. Rediscovering Jean was a great pleasure, but a Drew who terrified people? She was thoughtful as she hurried wardwards.

Colin Montrose's eyes were open quite half the time Annabel was treating him, though he certainly wasn't focusing properly yet. Minimal chest secretions and no adverse responses to full stretching of all muscles and joints not immobilised in plaster suggested no particular residual problems. He'd be unsteady on his feet at first, of course—she'd have to start him off in the parallel bars. That was if he wasn't turned over to the orthopods first. . .

Donnie Helm was something else. He was very rigid, and Annabel didn't care at all for the primitive patterns of muscle tone she was picking up. Step up passive movements to four times daily, then. And she'd better check on his medication to see if he was having anything to help reduce his spasm. Still, as Drew had observed yesterday, he had youth on his side. . .

Seonaid McLeod next. As Drew had predicted, her movements were erratic and wild. Treatment in front of a big mirror should help her, once the wee lass was completely with it. Another week or so, perhaps?

The back patients insisted that they never had their exercises before their elevenses, so Annabel looked in on the Walker sisters next. First Claire, the elder, with her left-sided stroke. Her main problem was abnormally high muscle tone hampering her movements. Ten well-spent minutes reduced that, but Claire was so delighted that she moved far too enthusiastically, and her tone shot up again. More reducing measures to correct, more movements, more carefully carried out, advice on how not to trigger spasm, then some walking practice. . .

'That's the furthest I've walked to date,' Claire told Annabel in conclusion.

'Great! But promise me you'll not try walking by yourself yet. Your balance isn't good enough.'

'I promise.' Claire subsided carefully into her chair. 'You've treated a lot of patients like me, have you not?'

With a wry smile, Annabel admitted to one or two, and Claire said she could tell by the way Annabel had handled her. The briefest of assessments was enough to show that Christine needed no therapy; something which naturally pleased both sisters.

It was good to leave one's patients happy, but a glance at her watch told Annabel it was now well after ten and she had only carried out four treatments. That was neurology for you. No wonder the admin people who didn't know a stroke from a sick headache were always querying the figures as compared with, say, general surgery.

Mrs Plockton next; she who was said to be so cheerful.

That was no exaggeration. 'I'll be gey glad when I can turn myself round without falling, Miss Kerr,' she trilled with much laughter, trying at the same time to demonstrate.

Annabel captured her in mid-twirl. 'You're not to do that. That's why Mrs Craig gave you this specially weighted walking aid with wheels.'

'But it's such a heavy wee devil to push, quine.'

'Thank goodness—that's just what it's supposed to be. Hold on tight and lean hard, then you'll not fall, and the effort of pushing will steady you up as well.'

'You're not wrong, are you?' chuckled Mrs Plockton after some practice. 'Am I getting the hang of it?'

'Beautifully, but you're still inclined not to think carefully enough before you move.'

'I'll try, lass. You've been so patient, I'd like to do that for you.'

'For us both, Mrs Plockton. See you later.' Half-past eleven now, so no time for coffee because the backs would be waiting. . .

'That was really great!' was the unanimous verdict after the class, when Annabel started them off, each on his own individual exercises. Surely she would be nearly up to schedule by the time she finished in this ward?

'Miss Kerr?' It was Michael Simpson, the fresh-faced young houseman. 'Do you mind if I ask you something? I've just seen a patient down in Casualty with cervical spondylosis and referred root pain. I'm getting them to fix him up with a collar, but I was wondering if you'd mind telling me what treatment I should write him up for. I know a lot of the chaps just write "Physiotherapy" on the referral cards, but Mr Maitland says that looks amateurish.' By now he was actually blushing.

Annabel smiled, remembering Jean's words and also how awful it felt to be newly qualified and uncertain.

'I'd need to see the X-rays, Doctor,' she reminded him gently.

'That's what I thought, so I brought them with me.' He took them out of the heavy manila envelope and held them up to the light for Annabel to read.

'I don't think you could go far wrong with some short wave and gentle neck traction in flexion,' she suggested after a moment.

'Gentle traction in flexion,' he repeated thoughtfully. 'Thanks very much, Miss Kerr, I'm very grateful.'

'Not at all—any time.' Annabel dimpled. 'There'll be a fee, of course.'

'Of course.' He thought about that. 'How about coffee and a Mars bar after lunch some time—Annabel?'

'That should just about do it—Michael,' she returned, lips twitching. They were both laughing when Drew Maitland said coolly behind them, 'Good morning. I hope I'm not interrupting anything important.'

Michael scuttled away without a word, leaving Annabel to face the music, if any. 'Not at all,' she returned serenely. 'I've finished my treatments—and my discussion with Dr Simpson. I didn't hear you come in,' she added.

'I'm not surprised, with all that merriment going on. Now then. Sister said something about Mr McEachern's wound. Do you know anything about it?'

'Yes, it's inflamed and leaking a bit, so I restricted him to static work for flexors and extensors today.'

'That sounds very sensible.' Drew went over to the patient and Annabel returned to her note-making. He had brought a dressing-tray with him to dress the wound himself after he had dealt with the trouble. Annabel reflected that most surgeons would have sent for a nurse to do that. He returned to her side to explain, 'One infected stitch was causing all the trouble. I've removed it, dusted liberally with streptomycin powder and taped it over. Another day of your conservative treatment and he should be ready for something a little more vigorous.'

'Thank you, I'll remember, Mr Maitland.' Annabel closed her file and left the ward.

Drew followed. In the corridor, he asked, 'How are you settling down, Annabel?'

He'd asked her more or less the same thing last night, or had he forgotten? 'Very well, thank you. It's so nice to be working with patients again.'

'You're not missing the teaching, then?'

'Not yet anyway.' Because he seemed to be having difficulty deciding what to say next, yet showed no sign of moving away, Annabel said brightly, 'Please, Mr Maitland, could I ask you to have a word with Mrs Plockton? I've impressed on her the necessity of using her aid every time she walks, but a warning coming from you would be more effective, I'm thinking.'

'Certainly I'll speak to her if you think it will help,' he agreed stiffly. 'But she's not merely cheerful, you know. She is also euphoric and therefore somewhat unrealistic about her abilities.' Then he walked away in the direction of Mrs Plockton's room.

Annabel watched him enter and close the door. He hadn't liked her laughing with Michael Simpson—and he had winced noticeably when she addressed him formally the second time. But what else had he expected? Especially with staff passing all the time. Nobody in the hospital would remember what they had once been to each other, and she certainly wasn't going to do anything to set tongues wagging.

When the door of Mrs Plockton's room opened, Annabel found herself scuttling round the corner, out of sight, like a startled mouse. Still there five minutes later?

She couldn't risk the perfectionist thinking she'd been wasting time! But the patients' lunch trolley was being manhandled out of the lift now, so Annabel returned to Physio.

Of course Miss Tannoch wanted to know how Annabel's first morning had gone, and having been told, she then added an unnecessary little homily on how to get on with one's colleagues. Annabel bore it stoically. There seemed to be only one colleague she might not get on with too well, and she doubted whether that particular complication was one with which her mentor had ever had to deal. Lecture over, Miss Tannoch asked Annabel what she was doing about lunch.

'I thought I'd just have a sandwich here, Miss Tannoch. Then I can go over my treatment notes for the afternoon session.'

'Then I shall join you,' decided the boss. 'It will be a chance to iron out a few little points.' Her eyes brightened. 'As you know, the canteen sandwiches are very uninteresting, but there's a nice little baker up the road who does lovely ones. So if you wouldn't mind going out, dear. . .'

Annabel said she didn't mind a bit.

'Chicken and ham salad is my favourite—and perhaps a strawberry tart?' Miss Tannoch was looking very sly.

Knows fine she's far too plump to be eating strawberry tarts, interpreted Annabel, while agreeing without a smile.

She found the shop without difficulty and made her purchases. Going back to the crossing opposite the hospital gates, she ran into Drew Maitland outside the wine bar. 'Hello there,' she said casually in passing, but he seized her elbow and brought her to such an abrupt halt that she dropped one of her paper bags. Simultaneously, they bent to retrieve it, banging their heads together. 'Rather late in the day for that,' observed Drew, a remark which made no sense at all to Annabel. He tossed the sticky mess that had been Miss Tannoch's strawberry tart into a convenient litter bin. 'I've ruined your lunch, so the least I can do is buy you another. I was just going into the Orange Grove anyway.'

'Thank you, but I can't possibly do that. You see——'

'Why not?' he interrupted brusquely. 'I thought we'd agreed on an amicable relationship.'

An amicable working relationship, she corrected silently. Aloud she said, 'I came out for Miss Tannoch's lunch as well as my own. We're going to discuss a few problems while we eat.'

'I see. Another time, then.'

Well, he had to say that, didn't he? 'Perhaps,' returned Annabel non-committally.

'But for the present, you must let me replace whatever was in that bag.'

'It was a strawberry tart for Miss Tannoch.'

Drew raised a satirical eyebrow. 'Well, well, well! And she a diabetic!'

'The naughty old thing!' breathed Annabel, vexed at how nearly she had helped her boss to do the wrong thing.

'I suspect her GP would describe her in rather stronger terms,' guessed Drew. 'Supposing you were to take her some fresh strawberries instead? You could tell her the baker was clean out of tarts.'

An impish smile broke over Annabel's expressive face as she said, 'Now that's what I call a really good idea.' She looked away then, because Drew was staring at her; there really was no other word for it.

'I'd almost forgotten how pretty you look when you smile,' he said slowly. Unwillingly too, she would have sworn.

But again she had felt that stupid little thrill. Was she mad? 'Do you happen to know the way to the nearest fruiterer's?' she asked briskly.

'It's quite near.' He would have taken her elbow again, but she stepped out of range. 'Please—you mustn't bother. I think I remember now.'

But just as he had ignored her protests when he paid for her supper the night before, so now Drew overrode her covert dismissal. He went with her to the shop, paid for the strawberries and saw her back to the crossing. 'Mind how you go,' he cautioned as they parted.

'I thought you'd been kidnapped or run over,' fluttered Miss Tannoch when Annabel finally returned.

'Nothing so dramatic.' Well, not quite! 'I had to bring you fresh strawberries instead of a tart, though.'

Immediately Miss Tannoch looked guilty. Did she guess she'd been found out? 'Never mind, dear, these will be delicious—and much less fattening.'

Lunch over, she would have kept Annabel back to discuss the material for the treatment-room's new cubicle curtains, but Annabel insisted gently but firmly that she had to see one of her patients most urgently.

On the way back to the unit, she fell in with Jean Fyvie who was also returning from lunch. 'You didn't show up for coffee and the head girl is very cross with you,' said Jean with mock ferocity.

'The head girl would have been even crosser if I'd not treated the patients properly, I'm thinking.'

'There's no denying that. Listen, Annabel, I found out over lunch that Sunday next marks Mr Strachan's tenth anniversary on the unit, and I thought it would be rather nice to have a surprise celebration for him.

Nothing elaborate—just an informal cheese and wine do at our house—but he's been very kind to us both over the years. My husband was his registrar before deciding that neuro-surgery was not for him and switched back to orthopaedics.'

'What a nice idea, Jean.' Annabel had not yet met the senior consultant, but he seemed to be generally liked.

'Yes, I'm renowned for my nice ideas. You are free on Sunday night, I hope?'

'I'm not sure. My mother is just about at the end of her tether, so I'm packing her off to friends in Edinburgh for the weekend, and she may not be back in time to take over.'

'But of course—your grandmother! I'm so sorry, my dear. Let's leave it that you'll come if you can, then!' said Jean as they parted outside her office.

Annabel went to treat Donnie Helm first. Treating him twice that morning had relaxed him somewhat, but she knew she couldn't let up. After Donnie, a lengthy session in the gym was required for the recovering head injuries, Messrs Cairns and McMahon. There would be some outpatients coming in too, and she simply must see Donnie again before she left. How would Miss Tannoch react if she put him on the evening list? It wasn't usual—chests only was the rule here, but then neither was Donnie's condition usual. . .

And so the afternoon was as busy as the morning, and when she heard the chink of teacups in Jean's office as she passed some time after four, Annabel was very glad to be spotted and invited in. Drew was there. The office was tiny and the only spare chair was right beside him, so Annabel perched on the windowsill instead. 'I love the sun on my back,' she said, noting his quizzical lift of an eyebrow.

'Was that your reason?' he asked. 'I thought you wanted the light behind you.'

'To hide the ravages of time? Thank you, but I don't believe I'm quite at that stage yet.'

'Whatever it may not have done, time has certainly polished up your repartee, Annabel.'

Jean stopped pouring out to stare at them. 'I think you two once knew each other better than I realised,' she decided.

'I think we probably did,' returned Drew, while Annabel was still racking her brains for some casual, throwaway remark. 'We met when Annabel had just left school and I was newly qualified. She was bursting with excitement about going off to physio college, and I was similarly ready to save the world. Otherwise, who knows what might not have happened?' He said all that so lightly that Jean began to laugh.

Not so Annabel. 'You haven't lost your touch,' she told him firmly. And to Jean, 'He was always fooling around, and nobody took him seriously,' she said, as she accepted a cup of tea. Surely that would put a stop to such provocation?

It did—at least for the time being. The talk turned to patients, and Annabel learned some useful facts that hadn't shown up in the case notes, and then with a glance at the clock Jean said she simply had to go and make sure that her two new nurses knew exactly how to turn and position unconscious patients.

'Do they not learn that in training school?' asked Annabel, not too keen on being left alone with Drew.

'Oh, yes, but I always check in case they've forgotten something. Help yourselves to more tea—there's plenty in the pot.'

'An excellent ward sister,' commented Drew as Jean left them.

'Remembering what a super head girl she was at school, I can believe that.' Jean's depature had left Annabel feeling rather nervous. That was something she hadn't felt for years, and she didn't like it. The tea was scalding hot, but she gulped it down as fast as she could, intent on getting away.

'You must have very poor sensation in your oesophagus,' reckoned Drew, observing her.

'No—just very little time to spare.'

'All the same, I would suggest that you slow down, or you could end up requiring plastic surgery.'

Annabel ignored that, drained her cup and replaced it on the tray. 'About Donnie Helm,' she said resolutely. 'He's extremely rigid and I was wondering whether he's having any relaxing drug, or whether what I'm picking up is the true extent of it.' She had already found the answer from the drugs chart, but she had to say something.

'Not as yet. I'm always loath to prescribe more medication than is absolutely necessary in these cases, but if you think it would enable you to get a better range of movement, then by all means he shall have something.'

'No, I can manage. As I said, I just wanted to be certain about the exact degree of rigidity, that's all.' Annabel was halfway to the door. Might as well give herself a pat on the back. 'As a matter of fact, I'm just going to give him his fourth treatment of the day.'

'I'm very impressed.' Drew had risen too, and had stationed himself in the doorway. 'I thought our chat last night in the Orange Grove had cleared the air, but you're still not at ease with me, are you, Annabel?'

For a split second she felt as if she was frozen. Then her first thought was to tell him childishly not to flatter himself. Finally she said deliberately, 'Oh, I wouldn't put it as high as that. All the same, I'd rather you didn't make any more remarks like that to Jean Fyvie or to anybody else. What's the point?'

'I thought we agreed to work amicably together.'

'So we did, but that needn't include raking up the past.' Especially as he apparently regarded as a joke something which had, at the time, been indescribably precious to her.

'If I've offended you, then I apologise.'

Offended? Not exactly, but hurt, unfortunately yes. 'I just think the past is best forgotten in the present context,' Annabel insisted quietly, shutting the office door behind her before Drew could answer.

When asked if Donnie could be treated by the evening physio for a few days while any improvement was charted, Miss Tannoch hummed and ha'ed, and finally asked Annabel what she thought would happen if everybody insisted on adding their pet patients to the acute chest list.

Annabel swallowed her indignation at such an unprofessional response and twisted the superintendent's arm a little, by saying she was only suggesting what was standard practice in other neuro-surgical units she had worked in.

Miss Tannoch then gave way as Annabel felt sure she would, but she insisted that Annabel must be the one to put it to the girls, who would not be very pleased.

They were a good bunch; Annabel expected no resistance and got none. Miss Tannoch was a dear in many ways, they insisted loyally, but she really was miles behind the times.

Just as last night, Annabel could see Drew in his consulting-room when she went to get her car. He appeared to be engrossed in the papers he was holding. Routine hospital stuff or the prelude to another late night of research? Anybody'd think he hadn't a home to go to, had been the opinion of the waitress Sharon. He had, but rather a noisy one, apparently. Why? At that moment, Drew looked up and their eyes met. Impossible to pretend he hadn't caught her staring, so Annabel raised a hand in a casual half-wave before diving into the car. She mustn't be caught out like that again. Yet what the hell does it matter? she was asking herself next minute. She was reading too much altogether into everything said and done. After all, what had really happened that afternoon? Nothing more than a consultant gently teasing one of his team. She'd experienced that a hundred times without getting so uptight about it. Why couldn't she view the present situation as calmly and with as little concern as Drew did? Damn Drew Maitland! Why the hell did he have to come back?

Annabel could tell that her mother had had a difficult day the minute she walked into the kitchen. Mrs Kerr was making pastry with a violence that wouldn't do much for the finished product and her eyes were suspiciously red. Annabel took the rolling-pin out of her mother's hand and pushed her gently on to a handy chair. 'Tell me,' she invited.

'It's not as if I don't consider her,' began Mrs Kerr with a gulp. 'I never do anything without getting her opinion first, only she doesn't stick with it. Sometimes I think the only thing to do is the exact opposite.' She dived into the pocket of her pinafore and pulled out a damp and crumpled hanky. She blew her nose, then went on, 'Yes, she will have her bath now. Then when it's drawn she insists she's already had one. So I do the washing instead, and then when the water in the hot tank's all used up, she wants to know why as she hasn't had her bath yet. It's the same with the food. "We've not had apple tart for weeks," she said half an hour ago. But I'll bet you my new blue blouse she'll not want this when it's baked.'

'Loss of short-term memory, rather than outright cussedness,' comforted Annabel.

'D'you think I don't keep telling myself that? But it doesn't help when it makes such a stramash of my day that I don't know whether I'm coming or going.'

'Don't let it, darling. Plan your routine and stick with it. Cook what you like, and if she asks for something else fob her off with excuses like the shops are shut and you haven't got the ingredients. The chances are she'll have forgotten all about it the next minute. Now off you go, pour yourself a large sherry and put your feet up while I finish the dinner.'

'That was quite delicious,' said Gran, wiping her lips delicately with her napkin after a second helping. 'Though I must say, it's the first time I've ever had apple tart for my breakfast.'

Disorientation in time was common now. Place and persons would surely follow soon. 'But it's nice to have a change, isn't it?' suggested Annabel. 'Now I'll go and get your morning paper and see if the post's come,' she added, meaning to give her mother a practical demonstration in handling confusion.

'What—at this time of day? Don't be so daft, lassie!' retorted her grandmother roundly. That particular episode hadn't lasted long!

Annabel didn't regret her own discomfiture, because the short exchange had brought a faint smile to her mother's pale cheeks. 'I'll go and light the sitting-room fire, then,' she offered peaceably. Surely Gran wouldn't find fault with that, now that the sun had gone round to the back of the house.

Later, with the fire going nicely and the old lady

slipping into her usual after-dinner doze beside it, Mrs Kerr said in a tired, quiet voice, 'Of course I realise I don't know much about these things, Annabel, but it does seem to me she's getting worse gey quickly. Old Mrs Dewar at the Post Office wasn't nearly so. . .' Her voice tailed off helplessly.

'Certainly it's usually the youngest patients with true Alzheimer's disease who regress most quickly, but there's always the exception to prove the rule,' Annabel whispered back. She sighed. Gran had always been bossy, but also she had always been very kind, and a tower of strength to them all in their vulnerable years after Father's desertion. 'I'm going to start keeping notes, Mother dear. Just in case there's something. . .' Annabel sighed again. Because what could anybody do to halt the inexorable downhill slide in these cases?

'Put on your coat and walk round the corner for a chat with Nancy,' she urged, naming the minister's wife, her mother's particular friend in Durless. 'I'll do the dishes and put Gran to bed—that's if she doesn't decide it's morning when she wakes up!'

CHAPTER THREE

SOMETHING big has happened, realised Annabel, as soon as she reached the wards next morning. Wednesday was operation day, but that alone couldn't account for the main corridor being as untidy as the fish market when the boats were unloading. Jean flashed past with her sleeves rolled up and a plastic apron protecting her dark blue dress. 'Accident,' she said succinctly over her shoulder before disappearing into the head injuries room.

That was where Annabel usually started work, but the little ward was already crammed to capacity with doctors, nurses, trolleys and a portable X-ray machine, so she would only be in the way. Claire Walker first, then.

But Claire and Christine had been moved out of their little room and in their place was a young man on the horribly uncomfortable-looking Streiker frame which was used for nursing patients with unstable spinal fractures. Almost, Annabel was wishing herself back in the quiet, cloistered regularity of the lecture-room. Dinnae be sae fushionless! she scolded herself as she went in search of her missing patient.

A very new student nurse, sore at being excluded from all the drama, was making beds single-handed in the women's ward, and she gave Annabel all the details. 'A helicopter taking some of the relief crew out to one of the rigs crashed on take-off. Most of the injuries were fractures—it must be frantic on Ortho!—but we've got three. There's a man in the side-ward where the sisters

41

were,' a jerk of the head across the ward located them, 'and two head injuries. One's not too bad they say, but Mr Maitland took the other one to theatre at seven this morning. Then he went and arrested about ten minutes ago—the patient, not Mr Maitland,' she explained painstakingly, unaware that she had said anything remotely humorous.

'No wonder the place is so chaotic,' commented Annabel, straight-faced.

'That's right. Goodness knows when they'll finish the theatre list today. They haven't even started yet. Isn't it exciting?'

'That's certainly one way of putting it! Wait a minute—you mustn't do that by yourself,' Annabel protested as the girl prepared to turn a mattress. 'You'll give yourself a PID. Now then—ready?'

Together they flipped the mattress over and the nurse asked wide-eyed, 'What *is* a PID, Miss Kerr?'

'A prolapsed intervertebral disc. No good to a nurse, that.'

'No, I suppose not. Actually, I'm not all that sure. . .'

Annabel whipped out her notebook and drew two lumbar vertebrae sidways on, adding a rubbery-looking protrusion, pressing on the nerve root.

'That looks very nasty,' breathed the student. 'No wonder it's painful!'

'Absolutely, so no more heroics. Promise?'

'You've got it.'

Nearly nine and nothing done yet, worried Annabel, as she crossed the ward to treat Claire. Still, if I've saved one over-conscientious wee nurse from doing in her back, the time hasn't been wasted.

Claire was very unsteady that morning; unsettled by the move, no doubt. 'Anybody'd think you were drunk,' said her sister with a giggle when Annabel lowered

Claire into her chair after the walk that always concluded her treatment.

'Cheeky besom!' considered Claire. 'It could have been you lurching about like this if I hadn't had the bad luck to pop my aneurysm before they found yours. Think of that!'

Annabel left them wrangling good-naturedly and went to find Mrs Plockton. For once she wasn't reeling round her room, so that pep talk Drew had given her must have made an impression. 'I'm trying to be good, quine,' she greeted Annabel, 'but it's awful hard. I'm not one for thinking first.'

First, lots of practice in standing up and sitting down, with Annabel resisting every movement. 'My son says that if I was on a planet with six times the weight of our gravity, I'd manage fine. He's a physicist,' Mrs Plockton added proudly.

'And a very clever one, by the sound of it. Now then, by yourself, Mrs Plockton. Careful, now—careful. I think I'll ask Mr Strachan if you can go to the hydrotherapy pool. Fighting the water'll slow you down no end.'

Still a lot of bustle in the HI room—it would be a miracle if she got Donnie treated twice that morning. But that was the way it went, according to the clinicians. New and more serious patients pushed the others down the scale of priorities, thought Annabel, rounding a corner and almost colliding with Drew. A shared second's staring and then, 'The new patients—Jean will brief you. I'm late for Theatre,' he rapped out, sweeping past. No white coat, shirt sleeves rolled up, tie loosened and his collar unfastened; somehow he looked younger like that, almost the eager boy she had once loved so completely. Annabel stared after him with a lump in her throat and a catch of the heart. God, but this was stupid! Unconsciously, she stiffened up as she marched on to the back ward.

'But we've not had our elevenses yet, Miss Kerr,' they greeted her plaintively.

'Sorry, lads, but the place is in uproar today—or hadn't you heard? Now then, duvets off and only one pillow apiece—Mr McEachern, no more than you did yesterday. . .'

The backs treated, Annabel went to the HI room, where all was now peaceful, except for the blip blip of the ventilator supporting the new patient who had arrested so dramatically.

Seonaid, Colin and Donnie were all much as they were yesterday. A quick look at the less serious of the new patients suggested that his problems were minimal—only kept in for observation then.

There was, however, the third emergency admission. Jean was in her office, wrestling with the paperwork she hated. 'You'll be wanting to know about the chap in the side-ward,' she realised with the acumen of the experienced ward sister.

'Please, Jean—if you're not too busy.'

'Unlike some strange people not a hundred miles from here, shuffling paper about is not the whole point of my working day.' Jean's lips tightened. 'Ian Buckie has sustained a rotational fracture injury at the D2/3 level.'

'Oh, lord!' The two girls stared at each other for a fraught moment as each contemplated the gravity of that.

'Miracle number one was the fact that he survived the accident, never mind the journey to hospital,' said Jean. 'Miracle number two was Drew Maitland getting him on to the frame without displacing the fractures. It was one of the neatest pieces of work I've ever seen.'

'So he's got a chance.'

'He has, but woe betide anybody who drops so much as a feather within ten yards of him for the next six weeks.' A great exaggeration, but Annabel got the point. The man was all right, as long as there was no gross disturbance of his metal cage. 'I'll not need to be telling you how to treat him, will I?' Jean continued. 'That's a point Drew made earlier. "I'm glad that somebody of Annabel's calibre is here to handle this," were his exact words. He thinks very highly of you.'

'Only because I stuck my neck out and wrote that treatment manual last year,' Annabel insisted.

'Perhaps—perhaps not. Just how well did you know him, Annabel?'

This was getting too close for comfort. 'About as well as any other temporary nursing orderly gets to know the houseman, I suppose. I do remember he was a terrible tease; nobody took him seriously. Are Mr Buckie's films about, Jean?'

'Over there, on the viewing screen.'

'Thanks.' Annabel switched it on and delivered a learned dissertation, which effectively drowned Jean's efforts to continue her probing.

'It's easily seen where your true vocation lies,' Jean observed drily when Annabel paused for breath. 'Did your students ever get the chance to ask a question?'

'Of course—providing it was relevant.'

'Point taken,' said Jean with a tiny smile, leaving Annabel with the realisation that she had fuelled her friend's curiosity, rather than dousing it. 'How about a quick coffee?'

'I'd love one, but I'm dreadfully behindhand this morning.' Which was a cast-iron excuse Jean couldn't possibly doubt on a day like this.

* * *

By giving up most of her lunch hour, Annabel gradually caught up, except that she'd only managed to fit Donnie Helm in three times, instead of the four she had set herself as a target. She looked at her watch; it was getting on for six. She'd only treated him an hour ago, so there was no point in disturbing him again so soon— and he would be on the evening list.

I'm still thinking like a teacher, she realised. Physio-therapy the centre of the stage, with everything by the book and no hold-ups, owing to the necessary input of other professionals. No emergencies, no visitors, no overloaded casebooks—nothing to interfere with the perfect plan. But Donnie wasn't going to be crippled for life, just because she'd had to miss out twenty minutes of treatment that day; he'd still had an hour. I've got to be more adaptable, she was telling herself as she looked into the office to tell the junior sister she was going off duty. Jean had left on a so-called half-day two hours before.

Sister Watson wasn't there, but Drew Maitland was. And obviously newly out of theatre, with a white coat shrugged on hastily over loose threatre-green cotton trousers and tunic. He looked hot and weary and was probably both. Annabel retreated, but he called her back. 'A warning,' he said, throwing down his pen and leaning back in his chair. He stretched aching arms sideways, then relaxed.

'Now what have I done?' asked Annabel, still smarting from her self-imposed sense of inadequacy.

His eyes widened. 'Why should you suppose you've *done* anything? I only wanted to warn you that you're going to be asked to do something you'll not want to do.'

'That sounds complicated. What exactly is this something?'

There was a tray of tea at his side and Drew filled the spare cup. Making room for it on the littered desk, he said, 'You seem somewhat fraught, so I'm prescribing the national remedy for stress.'

Annabel's face relaxed in a half-smile. 'Thank you. It sounds as if I'm going to need it. May I sit down?'

'Why not?' Drew picked up his pen again and absently doodled the outline of a brain on the message pad. 'You'll remember I mentioned our current research project?' She nodded. 'Well, in Theatre today, George Strachan was bemoaning the loss of Barbara's contribution, and it didn't take him long to decide on asking you to take over.'

'But I can't—not possibly!' she wailed.

'So you said, and that's why I'm telling you. Now you can be ready for him when he asks you on the round tomorrow—as he will.'

'It's not that I wouldn't *like* to. Simply that I haven't got the time.'

'Then you'd better prepare a good story. George is a very persuasive man.'

'Thanks for warning me.'

'Think nothing of it. And do drink that tea.' A slight pause and Drew added slyly, 'I thought you liked it scalding hot.'

Annabel half choked on a mouthful. Damn him for that! 'I was—preoccupied.'

'Aren't we all?' he asked with a sudden probing glance which couldn't have anything to do with her, could it? All the same, it made her feel rather uncomfortable.

'The new patients,' she said desperately.

'I was coming to them. How much do you know so far?'

'Jean told me all about Mr Buckie and I've treated him the regulation twice. Nothing untoward to report.'

'Let's hope it stays that way. You'll have gathered he needs the kid-glove treatment?'

'Oh, yes. I was extremely careful with him.'

'I don't doubt it. Now about the others. The lad Brown was just mildly concussed and will probably only be in for a few days, but Mr Ness is quite another matter. He sustained a depressed parietal fracture with extensive subarachnoid bleeding and he arrested in the ward shortly after arriving back from theatre, as you'll have heard. To put it kindly, he's rather a well-built chap who's a heavy smoker. And the chesty cold his wife says has spoiled his two weeks' leave is, in fact, a low-grade broncho-pneumonia. Am I going too fast for you?'

'No, I've got all that. Anything else?'

Drew smiled crookedly. 'Why? Isn't that enough?' Immediately he was serious again. 'I was reasonably satisfied with what I was able to do for him at operation, but the cardiac arrest raises questions. Was it solely the result of his head injury—which is severe—or does he also have some coronary artery disease, secondary to his heavy smoking? Also, is his pneumonia a primary or a secondary manifestation? Those questions must be answered as soon as possible. Either way, he's going to keep us all very busy for a while.'

'Would you like him put on the evening chest round?'

'Ideally, yes, remembering the pneumonia. But in view of the arrest, we'd better rely on routine suction only for the present and review him tomorrow. Nothing's ever straightforward, is it?'

'Only in the books, as I'm fast rediscovering,' returned Annabel.

Drew chuckled in a curiously throaty and attractive way which awoke old and painful memories as he reached for another biscuit. 'You've already eaten them all,' she observed unsteadily.

'That must be because I hadn't time for lunch. Actually, I'm feeling a trifle faint,' he added drolly. 'Perhaps a visit to the Orange Grove is indicated.' He quirked an eyebrow. 'I suppose you wouldn't care to join me?'

'I can't. I've got a date!' remembered Annabel, leaping guiltily to her feet. Until that moment, she had quite forgotten Adam, who would by now be waiting patiently at the hospital gates.

'I'm so glad that your grandmother's not taking up all your spare time,' returned Drew in an expressionless voice as Annabel said a hasty 'goodbye' and hurried out of the office.

Fifteen minutes later, after a lightning change of clothes, she dashed through the hospital gates and breathlessly asked Adam how long he'd been waiting.

'Not very long,' he returned kindly. 'I dare say you've been very busy.'

'Yes—today was rather hectic.' What an understatement! She was looking round for Adam's Audi. 'But where's the car? Did a traffic warden move you on?'

'Knowing you would have yours, I came in by bus, Annabel. It would have been—well, rather an anticlimax to go home separately, wouldn't it?'

Annabel began to laugh. 'Oh, Adam, what a pair we are! I came in by bus too, thinking this would be a good opportunity to get my car serviced.' She stopped laughing when she saw his expression of displeasure and hurt pride.

'I had intended that we should have our dinner at Pierre's,' said Adam heavily, naming Inverdon's priciest restaurant. 'But that's miles from the concert hall and quite out of the question now that we must rely on taxis.' He nodded across the road towards the Orange Grove. 'That looks quite a decent place.'

'Oh, no!' Drew would be there.

'The food is poor, then, is it?'

Too late, Annabel realised that a simple 'yes' would have been the thing. Instead she answered, 'Actually, it's not bad, but it's always full of hospital staff.'

'So? I don't mind if you don't.'

Now he's hurt because he thinks I don't want to be seen with him, she realised. She had had no idea that Adam was so sensitive, but, although he'd been around for most of her life, she was realising now that she didn't really know him. 'I only meant to warn you that it'll probably be rather crowded,' she offered placatingly.

'But there's no harm in looking, is there?' returned Adam, steering her firmly towards the crossing.

The place was, in fact, half empty. 'Plenty of room, after all,' he observed triumphantly. 'So where shall we sit?'

Annabel opted for a dark corner, but Adam said he liked to see what he was eating and chose a table near the window, where Drew couldn't fail to see them if he should come in. So what? What harm could come of her being seen by him with somebody as personable as Adam? But that wasn't the issue. It was her own reactions Annabel didn't trust. Was it really only two days since she'd faced up to Drew without a qualm?

Sharon greeted Annabel like an old friend. 'Busy day, quine? I'll bet, what with the crash and all.' She awarded Adam's rugged dependability and expensive tweeds a look of frank admiration. 'And I see you've got yourself a new man the night. Now then, the lobster pâte's awful good. . .' she paused, pencil and pad at the ready.

Their choices made and Sharon away, Adam asked

inevitably, 'What did she mean by that impertinent
remark?'

'Not impertinent—just friendly,' returned Annabel,
ducking the issue. 'Sharon always takes special care of
anybody from the Royal.'

'Even to the extent of noticing who they come here
with.'

Annabel sighed. 'As you know, I was on call on
Monday, so I came here for a meal to tide me over. The
place was packed and I had to share a table with one of
the doctors, that's all.'

'I wasn't prying, Annabel,' said Adam primly.

What, then? Oh, dear—Annabel couldn't recall being
so irritated with him ever before. This evening had
begun badly and looked like getting worse. She leaned
forward and gave him the smile which Chris, her final
London boyfriend, had said could melt the Berlin Wall.
'Did you buy anything at Forfar market yesterday,
Adam?'

'Actually, I was selling, not buying,' he corrected. Of
course he would be; Adam's prize cattle were coveted
the length and breadth of Scotland. But at least she'd
got him started on his favourite subject. Never mind
that, most of the time, she hadn't the faintest idea what
he was talking about!

The place was filling up now, and overheating, but
the temperature between them was also improving.
Adam loved talking about his famous herd and he was
also enjoying his meal; not to mention Annabel's company, now that she was proving to be such a good
listener. He rewarded her by covering her hand with his
own and giving it a painful squeeze, just as Drew edged
past on his way to the only vacant table. Which *had* to
be next to theirs.

Annabel fancied that she could feel Drew's eyes

boring into the back of her neck all the time she was toying with the large wedge of gâteau Adam had ordered for her without asking first. She would really have preferred some of that crumbly Stilton he was relishing, but Adam had the firm idea that women always went for something sweet. When he suggested coffee, Annabel said quickly that there might not be time as they didn't have a car. The back of her neck must be fiery red by now; not a happy contrast with her thick coppery hair. Adam agreed, so Annabel volunteered to go outside and try to find a taxi while he paid the bill. With luck, having one waiting by the time he came out would ensure the continued success of the evening.

Adam had secured two of the best seats in the concert hall, and he fussed Annabel into hers with a programme and a large box of chocolates. 'Oh, Adam, you're spoiling me!'

'If I am, it's only because you deserve it,' he insisted solemnly.

'Deserved or not, I like it very much!' Annabel took a nostalgic look round at the faded Victorian splendour. The lights were being lowered and now the performers were coming on to the stage. They had only just made it.

'Are you enjoying this?' asked Adam at the interval.

'Oh, yes. I adore chamber music.' Just as she had once adored the man who had introduced her to it.

'I prefer a good play myself,' revealed Adam.

'Do you?' How little she knew about Adam's preferences. 'Then why——'

'Because I knew this was the sort of thing you enjoyed,' he returned with heavy gallantry.

'You're so thoughtful, Adam, but I like the theatre too.'

'Then perhaps you'd like to go to the Rep on Saturday night? They're doing *Abigail's Party*.'

'I saw that in London some time back,' remembered Annabel. Sensing his disappointment, she added hastily, 'But I'd love to see it again. It's an absolute scream.'

'Then it's a date,' said Adam with an unexpectedly killing glance that sat uneasily on his earnest features.

'Except—Adam, I can't!' I'm packing Mother off to Edinburgh for a break this coming weekend.'

'I'm sure my mother would spend the evening with Gran.'

'But doesn't she play Canasta with the Baird sisters on Saturdays?'

'Yes, but they're friends of Gran's too, so they may as well meet at Rowan House.'

'Well, if they will——' Annabel began, just as a couple from Durless came up to speak to them. They made no secret of their interest at finding Annabel and Adam there together. Kirsty Reid was a champion chatterbox, so it would be all round the district within twenty-four hours. Annabel began to feel rather pressured. It was one thing to consider encouraging Adam, and quite another to have a relationship assumed and taken for granted.

At the end of the concert, Adam could hardly wait for the applause to die away before getting to his feet. 'You hated that,' guessed Annabel as they edged sideways along the row.

'As long as you enjoyed it, that's all that matters.'

'And I did—very much.' That was perfectly true, only—only what? 'It's only five minutes' walk to the bus station,' she said hurriedly, to drown out memories of coming here with Drew.

Adam looked at her as if she'd suggested going home by camel. 'I told that taxi-driver to come back for us.'

'Oh, Adam, how extravagant!'

'Possibly, but a preferable alternative.'

Should I offer to go halves with the fare? wondered Annabel for one mad moment, as she climbed into the taxi, duly waiting. Because she couldn't help feeling that the car mix-up was mostly her fault; or rather that Adam thought so. And she had thought this was going to be a straightforward and undemanding evening!

'You're very quiet,' observed Adam, tucking his arm through hers.

'Work—I was thinking of work,' she invented to take her mind off the ticklish issue of the taxi fare. 'We've got some of the casualties from last night's helicopter crash.'

'I heard about it on the local radio. Nasty business.'

'Yes, isn't it dreadful? One poor man has a badly broken back, though we hope he won't be paralysed, and another has a nasty skull fracture. He'd already got pneumonia, and then he had a cardiac arrest, which is making it very difficult to get the infected sputum off his chest. . .' Adam had withdrawn his arm and, by the light of the street lamps, Annabel would have sworn he had turned quite green. So her work was a topic she'd better not raise again. And yet Adam could probably do something equally messy, like delivering a calf, without turning a hair. Impulsively, she asked him.

He was astounded. 'What? Certainly not; that's a job for a vet. Why in the world did you ask me that?'

'I was only trying to take an interest in *your* work,' she answered in a small voice.

'Annabel!' His arm went right round her this time, and the rest of the way home he talked about selective breeding.

'Thank you very much for a lovely evening,' said

Annabel politely when he had walked her to the front door.

For answer, Adam took her gently by the shoulders and kissed her. It was comforting, even pleasant, but it raised no ripples. She watched him stride down the main street, his broad, stocky figure casting a shadow in the light of the setting moon. There had been several dates with Adam, but this was the first one that hadn't gone very well. She hoped Saturday's would be better.

CHAPTER FOUR

A QUICK tour of the chesty patients, and Annabel was ready to join the cluster in Jean's office, awaiting the chief. Drew was already there, and his only acknowledgment of her entry was a cool stare and a brief nod.

At first sight, Mr Strachan looked more like an absentminded academic than the eminent neuro-surgeon he was, but the gimlet gaze he cast over Annabel was anything but vague. 'So you're the girl wonder from St Crispin's,' he said at last. 'I must confess that your track record led me to expect somebody much older.'

Some sort of reply seemed necessary, so Annabel said modestly, 'Perhaps it's just that I'm wearing well, sir.' That successfully broke the ice, and the ward round began on a gust of laughter.

They took the route followed on Annabel's first day and began in the recent head injuries room. Mr Strachan listened stolidly to Drew's recital of their newest patient's injuries, subsequent crises and all the measures taken. Then he examined the man for himself. Afterwards, he turned a grave face to his entourage. 'I have to say that, frankly, I'm not hopeful.' They'd all been holding their breath while waiting for his verdict and now a series of sighs ran round the tense little group. 'But I've been wrong before in similar situations, so let's hope I'm wrong again.' He turned to Drew. 'One thing is sure—nobody could have done more than you did. Well done!' He gripped Drew's shoulder briefly, then put his hand to his head and stood looking down for a few seconds. It was as if he was at pains to clear his mind and leave it free for full consideration of the next problem. Then he moved on, with the retinue following.

'Any change here?' he asked, staring thoughtfully down at Donnie Helm.

'There was a minimal rise in conscious level two days back, but since then he's remained constant,' Drew reported.

'You'll have tested for any increase in intra-cranial pressure, of course.'

'That's constant too. There's been no more leaking of either blood or CSF.'

'Good. No pressure sores, Sister?'

'None, sir,' Jean returned woodenly, but there was a fiery flash of indignation in her bright blue eyes. The very idea!

'And what do you make of him, Miss Kerr?'

'He's very rigid, sir, but I'm managing to contain it with frequent passive movement.' Annabel hesitated. 'Actually, I was wondering if I might try ice. Apart from its relaxing effect on muscle, it's sometimes quite helpful in raising conscious level.'

'I don't doubt it. If somebody were to smother me in ice the way you girls do some of your patients, I think I'd wake up PDQ—no matter how profound my slumbers. Seriously though, I think that's a sound suggestion, do you not, Drew?'

'Undoubtedly.'

Annabel thought Drew had sounded rather put out. Did he think she was trying to upstage him, or did he have another reason? Yesterday afternoon he had seemed quite friendly, but this morning. . .

'. . .as soon as possible, then,' Mr Strachan was saying. 'Now what about our Colin?'

'Coming to nicely and aware about forty per cent of

the time,' Drew reported. 'I should be able to close off his tracheostomy in a day or two—and Seonaid's too.'

'Any intellectual impairment?'

'I think it's too early to tell, but I would doubt it. The biggest drawback to his rehabilitation is going to be his fractured tibia. The orthopods don't want him weight-bearing for another eight weeks. They'll be taking him over as soon as we're satisfied with his mental state. I thought towards the end of next week.'

Mr Strachan nodded. 'Fine. Now where is our Seonaid, Sister?'

'In the big ward, sir. We transferred her when Mr Ness was admitted. She knew there was something going on and I didn't want her upset.'

'Quite right. Now then, didn't you tell me there were two head injuries admitted yesterday?'

'He's also been transferred, George,' supplied Drew. 'He was only mildly concussed and he's quite lucid today. I looked at him before the round. He can probably go home tomorrow or Saturday.'

'Why not today, sir?' asked Bill Tait, the registrar.

'Because of the circumstances surrounding his injury,' explained Drew. 'I know what it says in the book, but we must be sure he isn't suffering from delayed shock before we discharge him.'

'The books are all very well, Tait, but there's nothing like experience,' supplemented Mr Strachan. 'Now then, I think it's time you showed me your miracle patient, Drew,' he decided as they paused outside the room the sisters had had to vacate yesterday. 'But first, show me the films and then we'll talk about him out here. No sense in letting him know what a narrow escape he's had. Plenty of time for that when he's ready to go down to the pub and impress his mates with the tale.'

'Quite remarkable,' considered the boss when Drew

had given him the details. 'Only minimal reduction of muscle power, you say? Amazing! But you're going to have your work cut out, are you not, Miss Kerr? A full assessment before the next round, if you please. You'll have briefed all your nurses, Sister,' he assumed confidently before going in to see the patient. 'Nice lad— great sense of humour,' he reported when he emerged. 'But that could pose a problem. We can't have him laughing too heartily, as I've explained to him. Now what about my old friend Mrs Plockton? Have you managed to stop her hurling herself to the floor every five minutes, Miss Kerr?'

'She's been much more careful since Mr Maitland gave her a little talking to for me,' returned Annabel diplomatically, earning a grudging half-smile from Drew. How nicely his grey eyes crinkled up at the corners when he smiled; she'd quite forgotten that.

Mrs Plockton demonstrated her abilities with only a few mild excesses brought on by the importance of the occasion. Mr Strachan decided that she could probably be discharged in about a fortnight, provided she went to stay with her daughter to begin with. 'Why is it that nearly all our elderly patients live alone?' he wondered as they moved on to the main wards. But nobody could provide him with an easy answer to that one.

As Saturday was Claire's baby daughter's first birthday, it was agreed that she could spend the weekend at home. 'And what about me?' asked Christine with a pout. 'Do I not get to my niece's party?'

'Sorry, but no,' said Drew with gentle decision. 'I want you right here until I'm quite sure that artery of yours is soundly healed.'

'But surely——'

'Shut up!' ordered Claire. 'You're going to do exactly what Mr Maitland tells you. You're not wanting to end up like me, are you, you daft quine? Even if I am improving every day.'

'Thank you, my dear. Perhaps we should make it a rule that every saucy young patient should be accompanied by an elder sister,' quipped Mr Strachan. 'Never mind, I expect they'll save you a slice of cake, lassie.'

Both Mr Cairns and Danny McMahon were declared to be slightly better than last week, though Danny was depressed. 'I think we should let him have Sunday at home, if his family are willing,' reckoned Mr Strachan, noting this. 'Best break a leg next time you decide to do yourself an injury, lad—you'll get over that a lot quicker than a gey great dunt on the head,' he concluded, bringing a smile to Danny's face as he had intended.

Annabel was assigned the new patients with Parkinsonism mentioned by Drew on Monday; together with a casual request for full assessments of their post-op state. 'You'll fit that in all right, will you not, Miss Kerr?' assumed their leader.

'No problem, sir.' Only that of finding the time, but what was the lunch hour for, if not for catching up?

Backs next, but before Annabel could follow the others into that section she was called to the phone. Miss Tannoch, sounding harassed, was wanting to know whether Annabel preferred yellow or green for the new curtains in the treatment-room. 'I'm being Pressured by Supplies,' she added, conjuring up a picture of a Mafia-style operation. Annabel suggested that yellow would brighten the place up and then hurried back to rejoin the round.

By then, though, it was over, so while they walked back to Jean's office for coffee, Drew joined Annabel at the rear of the procession and told her of the changes. 'Three for discharge and a new case from yesterday's ops list. Mary Kirk is a nurse on a geriatric unit, so no prizes for guessing how she came by her slipped disc. It was a huge protrusion and I'm not surprised she had some muscle weakness, as well as pain. Mr McEachern's wound is healed, so he can get going again now. Hey, where do you think you're going?' he asked as Annabel, having thanked him, would have walked on past the office.

'Back to the wards. I got so little done before the round.'

'Sorry, but your presence is required within. There's always a fair amount of discussion after a round—and don't forget my warning,' he added on a whisper as they entered.

'You'll have heard all about the research project, Miss Kerr,' Mr Strachan began at once. 'Mrs Craig will not be able to participate for a while, so we're hoping you'll stand in for her as capably as you're doing here.' Clearly he expected compliance.

'Miss Kerr has heavy family commitments, George,' interposed Drew, earning himself a grateful glance from Annabel.

'Haven't we all?' asked the boss. 'But there's really not a lot involved.'

Now where have I heard that before? thought Annabel wryly, recalling how similar projects used to snowball at St Crispin's. 'I'm very sorry to disappoint you, sir,' she said firmly, 'but things are extremely difficult at home, and, as that is the main reason for my leaving London, I cannot let my mother down now.'

No use. Mr Strachan knew what he wanted and how to go about getting it. Much against her better judgement, Annabel found herself agreeing to find out just how much was involved before turning down the idea altogether.

'Splendid,' said the two consultants as one. 'And as we're having a meeting in my room at five-thirty today,' added Drew, 'it would be very helpful if you could come.'

'Well, I don't know——'

'That's settled, then,' considered Mr Strachan, ignoring Annabel's witterings. 'Now has anybody any thoughts on my idea for changing round the wards? I really do think Sister. . .'

It was after eleven when Annabel finally escaped back to her patients. Donnie first, then the backs—heavens, there was the lunch trolley! Would it be feasible, just for once, to take Mrs Plockton, Danny and Mr Cairns as a group in the gym after lunch? That should leave time for one of those assessments. . .

'You're looking gey trachled, Annabel,' said Michael Simpson, coming out of the doctors' room to see her standing in the corridor with her hand to her head.

'Just wondering how to get the proverbial quart into the pint pot—in a manner of speaking,' she joked.

'I know the feeling, but you'll not get any more done here until they've all been fed, so why not come down to the canteen for some lunch? You've not collected your fee for that consultation yet,' he urged, noting her hesitation.

'You win. That's the best offer I've had for days, Michael,' she capitulated, laughing. 'So let's go.' She hadn't seen Drew come to the door of the doctors' room and stare after them, frowning.

'I feel ready for anything now,' reported Annabel when she and Michael returned to DSN after soup, salad and twenty minutes or so of relaxed chat.

'Told you that'd do the trick, didn't I?' crowed Michael. 'I wish I were off this weekend,' he added wistfully.

Annabel got the unspoken message. 'I'm on duty too, in a way. I'll be looking after my grandmother and she'll keep me on the hop, I can tell you.'

'She'll be the family commitment Mr Maitland mentioned. Some old people can be gey difficult, can they not? Be seeing you,' he added hastily, when Drew appeared in the doorway of Jean's office.

'Keeping busy?' asked Drew sarcastically. Michael had bolted, but Annabel stood her ground.

'There's certainly plenty to do, but I'm coping, thank you,' she answered calmly.

'And not only with the patients, it would seem. I do hope you'll not be too busy coping to come to that meeting later on.'

'I shouldn't think so—especially as I intend to work through the rest of my lunch hour.'

Determined not to let her have the last word, Drew retorted, 'As I invariably do,' before going back into the office and closing the door.

He was certainly in a bad mood today. And so much more serious than she remembered; there had been hardly a glimpse of the boy she had loved. Still, people changed, and he was probably under a lot of pressure— what with the latest serious cases, the research programme and his mysteriously noisy home conditions.

Despite her calm assurances to Drew earlier, Annabel was the last to arrive for the meeting. Coming across from Physio after changing out of uniform, she remembered that she hadn't let her mother know she'd be late, so she stopped off in Reception to borrow a phone. Having heard Annabel's explanation, Mrs Kerr said, 'That's quite all right, dear; now I'll not need to water the soup.' She went on to say that a one-time neighbour, back in Durless on a visit, had called in to see them and been pressed by Gran to stay to supper.

'How has she been today?' asked Annabel.

'The usual; with it and not with it by turns, and all at the speed of light. I'm doing what you suggested, though, and trying not to get too uptight.'

'That's the stuff! I hope I'll not be too late home. Now I simply must fly. . .' She arrived in Drew's consulting-room pink-cheeked and slightly out of breath.

There were four people there; Drew, the DSN registrar, a sulky-looking girl with dyed ginger hair scraped up in a bun on top of her head, and a giant of a man with a day's growth of beard and very sexy eyes. He looked Annabel over with insolent approval before saying in a lazy Australian drawl, 'You promised us brains, sport, but you never told us she was beautiful as well!'

Drew had been leaning against the wall, arms folded. Now he pushed himself upright and said brusquely, 'Annabel Kerr, meet Lisa Duncan and Jim Paul, our lab team. Of course you already know Bill Tait.'

Jim lounged over to shake Annabel's hand for far too long, while larding her with more compliments, to Lisa Duncan's obvious displeasure. Cleverly, Drew positioned Annabel and her new admirer on opposite sides of the room before opening the meeting.

'As you all know, some deep-seated brain tumours cannot be removed without permanent damage to surrounding tissue. I'll not bore you with operation procedures, but there is a new technique which I believe could minimise that.'

'Don't be modest, sir,' Bill Tait chipped in. 'We also know that procedure is your own idea.'

Drew acknowledged as much with a deprecating shrug. 'Anyway, to prove the point, it is necessary to reassess all patients operated on in the past by the current method, which is where Bill and Annabel come in. Then our future patients treated by the new method will be assessed for comparison.'

Despite her determination to remain detached, Annabel felt a surge of interest. Many lives had been saved by the removal of tumours, but sometimes at the cost of permanent disability. How wonderful if, in future, such patients could be restored to their former vigour!

Drew then went on to review the preliminaries, but he had noted Annabel's interest, and when the meeting broke up he said, 'I've some notes lying around here somewhere that I'd like you to read, Annabel. If you could hang on a minute, I'll find them for you.'

'Have a heart, friend!' protested Jim. 'Lisa and I are going over the road for a Foster's and we'd like Annabel to join us. How about it, Annabel?'

With Lisa looking daggers, Annabel opened her mouth to refuse, but Drew interposed swiftly, 'Great idea, Jim. I could down a half myself. You two go ahead and we'll catch you up.' It took him some time to locate the notes in question, and by then, Bill Tait had been called away. 'Now for that drink,' said Drew. 'Or better still, something to eat.'

Well, why not? It wouldn't be just the two of them. 'Lovely! I'm famished,' Annabel admitted frankly.

Drew raised an eyebrow. 'Even though you had lunch?' he queried, showing that he'd not forgotten she hadn't lunched alone.

The customary early evening rush was over and the Orange Grove was half empty. 'There must be some mistake,' protested Annabel, after looking round and failing to spot the others.

Drew thrust her into a corner booth before revealing, 'They'll be in the Pirate's Cabin up the road. The food there is lousy—guaranteed to land you in the ward beside Barbara. Anyway, you'd not want to play goose-berry, would you?'

'I understand,' said Annabel. The purpose of the delay was clear now. He'd been making sure the others got clean away. She'd been outwitted, and the only thing she could do was make the best of it. 'Three times here in one week?' she said lightly. 'They'll think I've got no home to go to.' Which was just what Sharon had said about him!

'Three times?' Drew enquired offhandedly.

If he was pretending that he hadn't seen her here last evening, then two could play at that game. 'Yes. Last night I went to a concert with a friend and we ate here beforehand,' she returned serenely.

'And which particular friend would that be?' Drew wondered. 'You seem to have so many.'

'Yes, I'm very lucky in that respect,' answered Annabel as Sharon appeared to take their order. She looked from one to the other, bright eyes assessing. 'Anything to drink?' she asked when they had both decided on chicken Kiev.

Drew ordered a wine that brought back vivid memories of similar meals years ago. He looked across the table at her, his expression bland so that she couldn't decide whether or not his choice had been deliberate. If only she could be sure she wasn't going slightly pink. . .'I'd better not drink anything, as I've got to drive home.'

'The half glass or so you declined on Monday'll not land you in the cells.' He paused, grey eyes scanning her face unhurriedly. 'Are you too warm? Would you like a window opened?'

Of course her flush deepened at that. Dammit, she hadn't blushed like this since they broke up and she grew up! 'Thank you—that's very thoughtful,' Annabel returned evenly, slipping off her jacket. 'The fact is, I've got far too many clothes on. My years in the south must have made me forget that we also get decent weather up here!'

A look of admiration for her quick thinking passed over Drew's face. 'You make it sound like half a lifetime in exile.'

'It was all my *adult* life,' she returned quietly.

A slight tightening of the jaw before he said abruptly, 'You told George Strachan this morning that your grandmother's condition was your main reason for returning. Does that mean you had another?'

Oh, sure! Three failed relationships in quick succession—and all with doctors at St Crispin's—was just the thing to get a girl talked about. The general opinion was that she hadn't any heart, whereas it was confidence she lacked—thanks to the handsome, self-centred man sitting across the table from her now. 'Yes, it does.' Annabel paused, noting the flash of interest registering in the deep-set grey eyes. 'I was thinking of leaving anyway, before my sister's letter came. I'd allowed myself to get more and more involved in research and college projects, and my life was becoming—unbalanced.' What a stroke of inspiration to quote her third reason like that!

That had disappointed him, and he hadn't been able to hide the fact. 'Out of the frying-pan, then,' he returned with a slight frown.

'Exactly.' And in more ways than one, if I'm not very careful, decided Annabel, just as Sharon reappeared with their supper.

While they ate, they talked off and on about impersonal things, like recent changes in medicine and what the developers and the oil industry together were doing to Inverdon. Then over second cups of coffee, Drew suddenly asked, 'Do you remember the little café that was here before this place?'

A vivid picture of it—and of the two of them holding hands at their favourite corner table—came startlingly to mind. Annabel gulped, but kept her head. 'Of course, but this is a great improvement, isn't it? That place was really rather grotty.'

'Was it? I never noticed that.' A pause. 'I was always—too preoccupied,' Drew returned softly.

It was his first serious reference to the past, and Annabel was appalled at the strength of her reaction. It was alarming, depressing and humiliating to find herself still so vulnerable. When she had got herself together, she said, 'I remember that too. You were a raving workaholic even then.'

'Point taken,' said Drew quietly, turning to signal to Sharon for the bill.

Annabel took out her purse. 'My turn to get this, I think.'

He gave her a level, quelling look that had her putting her purse away, even before he said, 'That may be how they do things in London, but up here we're not yet that advanced.'

'So you're not working late tonight,' surmised Annabel, really just for something to say, when they had crossed the road and passed the main door of DSN in a not too comfortable silence.

'George is on call tonight.'

'And the research programme?'

'Despite your diagnosis of professional paranoia, it's still a fact that I like to relax occasionally.' He hadn't forgotten that thrust. 'But as you brought up the subject, does that mean you're giving it some thought?'

'I'm sorry, Drew, but two evenings a week, as well as

my on-call nights, would be too much along with my other commitments.'

'Such as going to concerts with friends,' he suggested coldly.

He *couldn't* be—no, of course he wasn't jealous! They had reached her car now and as she rummaged in her bag for the keys, Annabel answered, 'Believe it or not, I too like to relax occasionally. I shall write and tell Mr Strachan—politely, of course—that it's quite out of the question.'

'He'll not like it.'

'Too bad,' she said. 'But there's nothing in my contract about compulsory research.'

'He could make things unpleasant.'

He had her pinned right up against the driver's door now. Is he going to kiss me? she wondered wildly, suddenly awash with longing, self-disgust—an absolute welter of conflicting emotions. 'If he does, then I shall leave! Please—I want to get in. . .' Her frantic eyes fell before his level stare.

There was a tense moment, with their bodies touching and the feel of his breath on her cheek before he stepped back. 'I think we know where we stand now, do we not?' he suggested in a voice of deceptive gentleness. 'Thank you for your company tonight, Annabel. Drive carefully now—goodnight, my dear.'

He was away first, driving the big silver Volvo estate which she'd noticed as they passed DSN. Annabel sat on, waiting for calm. Just four short days had been enough to rekindle the attraction he had held for her; it was pointless not to admit that obvious truth. To herself only, though. She was warned now; she knew the danger. Never by look, word or deed would she be revealing her secret. Because if Drew had really loved her as she had loved him, he would never have let her go. Even now, there were still some things which could only be seen in black and white.

It was after eleven when Annabel got home and the Northern Lights were turning the deep purple night sky into a pop video when she parked in the yard behind the old house. She got out of the car. The air was cool, fragrant and pollution-free. So many compensations in return for giving up her prestige job. It was in her own hands to ensure there were no more disadvantages than the one she had come home especially to deal with.

She tried the back door, though fully expecting to find it barred, but it opened. 'Do you not think you should keep the back door bolted after dark, dear?' she asked her mother, when she found her reading peacefully in the sitting-room with her feet up.

'Nonsense, Annabel. Nobody breaks into houses in Durless. How was your meeting? And did you get something to eat?'

'It was too long—and yes, thank you, I did. I could do with a cup of tea, though. No, I'll make it—you stay put,' she ordered when her mother put down her book and swung her feet off the couch. 'Tell me first, though, how was Gran today?'

'As I told you on the phone, amazingly good. After May came, that is. She got it into her head that May was a new maid, and May went along with it. Gran had a lovely time instructing her in her duties—you never heard such a rigmarole, and she quite exhausted herself. After that, she went off to bed like a lamb, no bother.'

'I'm so glad.' Annabel kissed the top of her mother's greying head, and went off to make the tea. For once, it sounded as if her mother's day had been less emotional than her own.

CHAPTER FIVE

'ANNABEL! You're gey early this morning,' was Drew's greeting when they met at the foot of the staircase leading to their wards.

'So much to do,' she returned with a small smile. 'Anyway, you're not exactly late yourself.'

'Your reason is mine,' he said. 'There's an outpatient clinic this morning and I want to check on the ward patients first.' He paused. 'Have you written that letter to George Strachan yet?'

'There hasn't been time. Home late, away early. . .' Her voice trailed off. Sticking to her resolution on emotional concealment would be a whole lot easier if he weren't looking at her quite so searchingly.

'Was lack of time your only reason? You wouldn't be wavering, by any chance?'

Now why was he asking that, when only last night he had said that now they knew where they stood on this issue? 'Certainly not,' she denied firmly. 'My mother needs all the help I can give her.'

'I can imagine. But she'd not want to stand in your way. She's a most unselfish and understanding woman.'

That was true. Even to the extent of understanding Drew's point of view all those years ago, Annabel recalled now. She and her mother had had quite a row about that. 'Which is precisely why I haven't told her anything about the project. After all, if I wasn't going to help her, then I might just as well have stayed in London and not raised her hopes.' But precious little help I've given her this week, one way and another, Annabel thought guiltily.

'Do you wish you had?' Drew asked abruptly, a certain something in his tone.

'In many ways, yes.' At least she hadn't been in any danger of repeating old mistakes there!

He shrugged. 'Inevitable, I suppose,' he muttered as he pushed open the door of the RHI room. Annabel followed him in, glad of the chance to acquire the latest information. 'How is he?' she whispered when Drew had examined their newest patient.

He sighed heavily. 'Holding his own—that's all one can say.' His glanced strayed to the bed where Colin was grasping the cot sides and hauling himself up to look round, in spite of having one arm in plaster. With a twisted little smile Drew commented, 'There's one at least who is making progress.' His attention switched to Donnie Helm. 'Let me know how you get on with the ice packs, won't you? Now I'm going to take a look at Ian Buckie. See you.'

Colin really co-operated for the first time, though his attention span gave out before Annabel had finished his treatment. Donnie reacted quite strongly to the ice packs placed on his most contracted muscles. His conscious level was definitely up then. But Mr Ness remained oblivious to all her ministrations.

Ian Buckie was stoically realistic about his misfortune. The sheer bravery of so many people in the face of adversity gives the lie to all this talk about deterioration in moral fibre, decided Annabel.

Going down the corridor, she was astounded to meet Claire coming to meet her. 'Claire! What do you think you're doing?' was the normal reaction; then Annabel realised that the girl was walking quite safely with her stick. 'The prospect of a weekend at home seems to be more beneficial than any amount of therapy,' she observed wryly.

'I'm not saying it's not helping. How'm I doing?'

'Just fine—but don't get carried away.'

'I promise.'

Half an hour with Claire, the same with Mrs Plockton and nearly as long with one of her new post-op patients took Annabel nicely up to Back Time. Another morning away without time for a coffee with Jean, although judging by the way she'd been tearing about, Jean herself hadn't the time for such frivolities either.

Annabel was on her way to the canteen for lunch when she met Jim Paul. 'I was looking for you,' he said. 'Where did you get to last night?'

'It took Drew longer than he'd expected to find that literature for me, and then when we got to the Orange Grove, you and Lisa weren't there. Some mix-up about the rendezvous, I guess.'

'Mix-up, hell! The sly devil meant to keep you to himself.' He swept her with an undressing look. 'Not that I blame him. I'm a push-over myself for redheads—especially natural ones.'

Poor Lisa! Was that why she dyed her hair? Jim took it for granted that they were lunching together, and Annabel submitted, rather than cause a scene. This created quite a lot of interest and whispering at the physios' table—and at the table where the DSN team were lunching, Drew was frowning, while Michael Simpson's face was a study in dismay.

Conscious of Drew's scrutiny, and of the need—since last night—of creating a smokescreen, Annabel was nicer to Jim than she would otherwise have been. Unwise. She then had quite a job persuading him that she couldn't possibly go out with him that weekend, or any other time. 'Sorry, Jim, but I'm already spoken for,' was her final excuse, to which Jim asserted that he'd be glad to have it out any time with any guy who stood between him and a beaut sheila like her.

When Annabel returned to DSN, Drew was waiting for her. He called her into the doctors' room and said without preamble, 'I'd have thought you'd have more sense!'

Annabel knew quite well what he meant, but she put on an innocent face and asked mildly, 'About what, please?'

'Jim Paul is the best biochemist I've ever come across, but he's also the most ruthless womaniser.'

'I can believe that,' she returned, spiking his guns—or so she thought.

'Was that why you were openly encouraging him, then?'

She refused to rise to such provocation. 'Just being pleasant. After all, it's hardly my fault if the occasional man finds me attractive, is it?'

'That's a joke! You're knee-deep in besotted admirers, as far as I can see!'

'Thank you—you're doing wonders for my morale,' she was saying as Jean came flying in.

'Quickly! Mr Ness!' she panted, which was enough to send Drew dashing after her without a backward glance.

If Mr Ness was in crisis, then Annabel realised she must re-plan her afternoon, leaving Donnie until later. There was nothing she could do for Mr Ness, and those who could would need all the elbow room they could get. So she went instead to collect Mr Cairns and Danny for a session in the gym. Mrs Plockton too, why not? She'd thoroughly enjoyed herself yesterday and had made Danny laugh such a lot as well. Next, Annabel looked in on Nurse Kirk to see if she had cheered up at all since the morning. Her pain was better since her op, but she was worried because her leg still felt so weak. Annabel explained how much longer it took to regain muscle power and urged her not to worry. After that, being the only physio on the staff who had taken a post-graduate course in acupuncture, she had to return to the department to see an outpatient started on a course of treatment before this week's dramatic change of routine.

On returning to DSN, Annabel glanced into the RHI room and saw that Mr Ness's bed was empty. Back to theatre for more surgery was her reading, so she seized the chance to give Donnie his ice therapy. He wasn't focusing yet, but he did open his eyes with a most reproachful expression on his face each time she renewed the ice packs. 'We're all very pleased with you, my lad,' she told him.

What a mess using ice always made, despite every care. Annabel mopped up the puddles on the floor—thank goodness the bed itself was dry—then carried all her paraphernalia to the sluice for sorting. Next, a brief written report for Drew, who had asked to be told how Donnie responded. A one-to-one would not be wise, thought Annabel, so soon after their acrimonious exchange at lunchtime.

Emerging from the doctors' room afterwards, she saw Drew standing by the exit, with his arm around Mrs Ness's shoulders. Sheltered in the lecture-room, Annabel had almost forgotten the darker side of clinical work, but there was no mistaking the purport of that scene. She ran into Jean's office, which fortunately was empty, and dropped on to the nearest chair. Thank goodness Donnie had been her last patient—she couldn't have faced anybody else today in this state. She hadn't felt like this since her first week on Surgical as an orderly.

When somebody came in and shut the door, Annabel

sniffed and searched frantically in her tunic pocket for a tissue. A hand appeared over her shoulder, offering a handkerchief. 'Try this,' said Drew in a voice of infinite gentleness, which had the effect of freeing her tears.

'Th-thanks. I'm'—sniff—'behaving like a perfect fool.'

'That is a matter of opinion,' returned Drew in the same gentle voice. 'The day we stop caring what happens to our patients is the day we should quit.'

She turned round and gazed up at him. 'But how——?'

'I caught your expression just before you dashed in here. It's a long time since you had to face this, is it not?'

He understood! 'Oh, Drew—that poor man! And his family. . .'

'Have been spared a lot of misery,' he told her quietly.

Annabel stared. 'But how is that possible?'

'That pneumonia,' he said. 'I had my suspicions, so I got the anaesthetist to do a bronchoscopy while we had him in Theatre the night he was brought in. The report came back this morning. He had a carcinoma of the bronchus.'

'I remember your telling me he was a heavy smoker.'

'So now perhaps you can see that his head injury was a blessing in disguise. He's known nothing about anything since the crash and has been spared the knowledge that he was dying—as well as all the physical distress he would increasingly have experienced.'

'His wife must have felt a bit better when you told her that.'

'I hope—I think she did.' Briefly he laid a gentle hand on her shoulder, giving her a comforting squeeze. 'And do you?'

'Yes—thank you.'

'Tender-hearted little Annabel,' he said softly. 'And I thought you'd changed; grown hard and sophisticated with the years. I'm glad it was only a pose.'

'But I have changed,' she insisted. 'I've grown up, and my expectations of life are—much more realistic.'

'And your expectations of people?'

Annabel thought carefully about that. 'I try not to have any. That way I can't be disappointed, and then quite often I'm pleasantly surprised.'

He frowned. 'That sounds very cynical.'

'Yes, I suppose it does. But then we're all the product of our experiences, are we not?' she was asking as Jean came in and dropped into the chair behind her desk.

'Did neither of you think of putting on the kettle?' she asked exhaustedly.

But Drew had letters from that morning's clinic to dictate and Annabel wanted to hurry home and let her mother away for the weekend, so Jean said plaintively that if they were both going to desert her she supposed she'd just have to settle for a teabag in a mug while she wrestled with the off-duty rota.

Drew walked with Annabel as far as his consulting-room. 'Are you sure you're feeling better?' he asked kindly.

'Yes, I am,' she returned in a stiff little voice. She was cross with herself for having shown her weakness earlier. It had been a chink in the cool sophistication she felt sure she'd been projecting successfully until then.

'Never be ashamed of caring,' he said, reading her reactions again, just as he had when he offered her his handkerchief. 'Annabel——'

Embarrassed, she'd been avoiding his glance. Now she looked up at his tone of entreaty. 'Have a good weekend,' he said abruptly before going into his room and shutting the door.

Annabel was in a very thoughtful mood as she crossed over to Physio to change. Twice that day, Drew had read her thoughts, whereas she hadn't come close to gauging his mood. With her secret to guard, she had better be more careful in future.

Gran had had a bad day, which meant that Mrs Kerr had too. 'If it hadn't been for the thought of my weekend, I think I'd have run off and left her,' she confessed. 'Is that not wicked?'

'I don't agree,' said Annabel firmly. 'You're doing your duty by her and you'll go on doing it, but that doesn't mean you've got to pretend you're enjoying it. How could you?'

'Oh, Annabel, you're like a breath of fresh air! What would I do without you?'

'Aw, shucks—you're making me blush!' joked her daughter. 'Away with you now, and have a great time in the big city.'

Mrs Kerr was going to Edinburgh to spend the weekend with friends. 'But are you sure you can manage?' she worried.

'Yes, Mother, of course I am.' Annabel picked up her mother's case and carried it out to the car, standing ready at the kerbside. It was a glorious evening, with Durless dreaming gently in the sun, down in its little strath between two ranges of fir-clad hills. 'You're going to have a gorgeous drive, Mother,' Annabel predicted, opening the car door and bundling her mother in before she decided not to go after all, as Annabel knew she was quite capable of doing.

And so Annabel began her shift of Gran-minding. The old lady was her usual capricious self; charming and irascible by turns, with the occasional tearful and self-pitying interlude thrown in. Annabel kept notes, but observed nothing she wouldn't have expected, and, despite her determination to remain detached and objective, she was feeling quite frayed by the time Adam and the Gran-sitting party arrived early on Saturday evening.

No wonder she greeted Adam with such enthusiasm! Charmed and emboldened by this, he put an arm round Annabel's shoulders and kissed her on both cheeks. Quite unprecedented, that, with his mother and the little Baird sisters hovering wide-eyed on the sidelines.

They think we're a lot further on than we are, realised Annabel, suddenly becoming very brisk. 'Everything's ready in the kitchen for coffee and eats later on,' she told Agnes, while settling the three old ladies in the sitting-room. Gran, who five minutes before had been purring with pleasure at the thought of their visit, was now gazing at them in astonishment and demanding to know why they weren't in the kirk on a Sunday morning. Cravenly, Annabel left Agnes to sort that one out and ran upstairs to get her coat.

Adam handed her into his car as carefully as though she were a piece of Dresden porcelain. 'I think you're quite wonderful,' he said as they drove off.

Annabel interpreted this as referring to her sense of family. 'Not really; just paying my debts,' she returned lightly as she wound down the car window. 'Isn't this a perfectly lovely evening? Did you ever see the heather looking quite so dazzling?'

'Would you rather have gone for a drive, then?' he wondered anxiously. 'I dare say we could return the tickets and then go up Deeside—or over Cairn o' Mount.'

'You're very thoughtful, Adam, but I'm really looking forward to the play.'

'That's good, because so am I.'

Being Adam, he had been careful to arrive in good time, thus avoiding the problem of last-minute parking, so they were among the first to take their seats in the front row of the dress circle. 'How extravagant—and very nice,' said Annabel on discovering that.

'Nothing is too good for you, Annabel,' Adam returned earnestly.

A girl taking her seat further along the row slipped him a covetous glance. Yes, he is rather good-looking, discovered Annabel, after studying him covertly herself. When he turned his head and met her glance, she looked hastily away. Better not to send out too many messages. . .

She leaned forward over the parapet to study the folk filing in below. 'See, Adam? That woman down there in the yellow trouser suit has got an arthritic hip; I can tell by the way she's walking. And there's a man with his foot in plaster. I do hope he's got permission to put weight on it——'

'Don't you ever forget that you're a physiotherapist?' interrupted Adam with the merest trace of impatience.

'Not often. . .' Her voice tailed off because that man down there, edging along the row behind the reed-slim girl with the long dark hair, was unmistakably Drew Maitland. Annabel sat back quickly in her seat. I won't—no, I will not, she vowed. But somehow her hand found its way into her bag and extracted the coin needed to unlock the opera glasses fixed on the barrier in front of her.

The girl was gorgeous—no disputing that. And theirs was a long-standing relationship. Even at this distance, she could tell how comfortable they were together. Slowly Annabel replaced the glasses, conscious of Adam's questioning look.

'I just thought I saw somebody I knew,' she said bleakly.

'And did you?'

'I'm—not sure.' She opened her programme and pretended to be engrossed in the credits, while wrestling with the realisation that she'd been assuming Drew was still unattached. And wasn't there good reason for that? His lifestyle of work and yet more work couldn't leave much time for anything else. Now Annabel knew she'd been mistaken. So she'd almost certainly been mistaken about something else too. Drew's friendly overtures were not so much fuelled by tender memories as by the determination to secure her help with his research. Eight years on, and as gullible as ever. What a fool!

The play was performed with tremendous panache, if less finesse than the London production Annabel had seen. As they descended the main staircase to the foyer afterwards, Adam asked her what she had thought of it. 'I can't remember the last time I enjoyed a play so much,' she told him, because it wasn't his fault the evening had turned to dust and ashes.

'Honestly, Annabel? Not even in London?'

'Not even there.' Realising that Drew and his girl-friend or whatever were now only feet away from them, Annabel tucked her arm through Adam's and, gazing up at him, said in a carrying voice, 'Of course, it's the company that makes all the difference.'

She went on being nice to him all the way home, reaping the harvest of a smothering and clumsy embrace in the hall, once the front door was shut.

Agnes had heard them come in and she opened the sitting-room door in the middle of it, causing her son to leap backwards like a scalded cat. He collided with the massive old dinner gong, which protested with deafening sonority, bringing Gran shuffling out into the hall, wanting to know in a terrified voice if it was Judgement Day.

Getting her calmed down took some time, and by then the Baird sisters were casting frequent glances at the clock.

Adam had to take them and his mother home, without any chance of renewing his courtship.

CHAPTER SIX

ANNABEL had decided that she didn't want to go to
Jean's party. So it was unfortunate that Jean rang to
persuade her just as Mrs Kerr walked in through the
front door, because she got to the phone first. Relaxed
and cheerful after her carefree weekend, she promised
that of course Annabel would be there, as soon as she'd
grasped what it was all about.

'But, Mother, Gran's been very strange all day. She
woke with a terrible headache and I'd swear she didn't
know me, or where she was. She seemed a bit more with
it once I'd got her fed, washed and dressed, but then
somebody came to the door and I had to leave her for a
few minutes. When I got back, she was looking very
odd—rather like somebody who'd just had a fit.'

'Oh, Annabel! But that's not very likely, is it?'

'No, it's not, but she was certainly looking very
peculiar. Then this afternoon, she flew into a terrible
rage over nothing at all and started throwing things.'

'She's never done that before. Was anything broken?'

'Only a cup and that china shepherdess thing that
nobody's ever liked. So you can see why I don't think I
ought to leave you alone with her.'

'That's silly, because you'll have to when you go to
work tomorrow. Anyway, I've had my fun; now it's your
turn.' Mrs Kerr was adamant. 'So go and get ready at
once, or I shall wonder why you don't seem to want to,
when you've always loved parties.'

That would never do, in case Mother got to hear that

Drew was back. 'I'm on my way,' Annabel insisted quickly.

Now, with hindsight, she could see what a pity it was that she'd ever brought him home. But how could she have avoided it, with Mother and Gran so curious? And her home, unlike his, so near to Inverdon? Drew had told her something of his family; his widowed father, sister Shelley and strict aunt Maggie who kept house for them in the gaunt manse on one of the remoter Shetland isles. It had been understood that some time, when Drew got leave between appointments, he would take Annabel to meet them all, but the break-up intervened.

And now, not knowing that Drew was back, here was Mother packing her off to have fun at Jean's party!

Fun? Hardly, because by now Annabel had quite decided that the elegant raven-haired beauty who had been with him at the theatre last night was Drew's wife. For contrast, then, she would go for the demure maiden look. She pressed her green print Laura Ashley and looked out the Princess Di green court shoes with the floppy bows, before taking a quick shower.

She had been wearing a dress very like this the first time she and Drew ever went out together. Would he perhaps remember—even feel a pang or two? Not very likely, though he wouldn't be too comfortable about having his past and his present in the same room. Just supposing she were to drop a few careless words about those suppers at the Orange Grove? It was quite possible that Drew wasn't looking forward to this party any more than she was! Annabel began to feel better.

She took a lot of trouble with her appearance. More mascara than usual on thick lashes, a touch of blusher on high cheekbones, short sculptured cap of thick copper hair brushed and brushed until it dazzled. And finally, the last of the Arpège which Chris had given her for her birthday.

'Darling, you look absolutely fabulous,' considered Mrs Kerr with pride when Annabel was ready.

'Thanks, dear. Now there's cold chicken and a salad, and——'

'Be off with you!' ordered her mother, propelling her firmly towards the door. 'And if by chance Gran should get stroppy again, then I'll—I'll just send for the polis.'

Annabel smiled as she went to get out her car. Mother's weekend of freedom had certainly done wonders for her morale!

The Fyvies lived in a roomy, newish house on the western outskirts of Inverdon, and, judging by the packed drive and all the cars lined up on either side of the gate, she must be the last to arrive. Well, almost. There was no sign of the silver Volvo estate.

It was another glorious evening and the windows were wide open, releasing sounds of animated chat and bursts of laughter. Jean was crossing the hall to the dining-room with a large covered tray. 'At last! I'd almost given you up,' she cried when she saw Annabel. 'Coats first left at the top of the stairs, and you'll find Bob dishing out drinks in the lounge when you're ready.'

Having left her jacket and checked her appearance, Annabel was going downstairs again when she spotted Drew with Jean in the hall below. Almost without thought, she doubled back out of sight. Too late. Drew had seen her, and when she rounded the bend a second time, he was waiting for her. Now what?

'Good evening,' she said placatingly.

Drew didn't bother with such niceties. 'I don't bite, as you might well have remembered, so why the evasion tactics?'

If that wasn't a direct reference to the past, then Annabel didn't know one when she heard it. Don't forget the brunette! 'I—I forgot my hankie,' she returned with a straight look that dared him to disbelieve her.

'You seem to make a habit of that. Perhaps you should have it pinned somewhere about your person,' Drew suggested in a slightly less caustic tone.

'Thanks for the notion. I'll probably act on it,' said Annabel, adding a smile mostly for the benefit of a large lady enveloped in floral polyester, who was taking a great interest in their conversation.

Drew couldn't see that, being in front of her. 'Let's get something to drink,' he suggested, taking Annabel firmly by the elbow and steering her towards the lounge, where he introduced her to Jean's husband.

Bob Fyvie had one of those pleasantly ugly faces which inspired instant confidence. Annabel would have liked him on sight, even if he hadn't said with obvious sincerity, 'It's nice to meet you at last, Annabel. Jean tells me you and she are old school chums.'

'It's very nice of Jean to say so, when she carried off all the prizes and I sort of slipped through unnoticed,' she laughed, accepting a glass of punch.

'I don't believe that,' said Bob, handing Drew the straight Schweppes he had asked for. 'How are you finding the old place, anyway? Have you settled in all right?'

'More or less, but it's wonderful to have Jean's support.'

'Don't tell me the doctors are giving you a bad time,' returned Bob, turning a reproachful eye on Drew.

Drew all but choked on his tonic water. 'Quite the contrary. Every unattached male in the place seems hell-bent on giving her the time of her life.'

Bob having perforce turned away to dispense more drinks, Annabel reproved Drew gently, 'You seem much more inclined to exaggeration than I remembered.'

'On the contrary, I'm being very restrained. I could have said in and out of the place as well. Did you enjoy the play last night?' he asked to underline his meaning.

'Yes, very much, thank you.' Annabel paused for effect. 'Did you?'

She had meant to unsettle him by letting him know that the sighting had been mutual, but if she had he gave no sign of it. 'A certain amount of overacting by some of the cast rather spoiled it, I thought. What did your *friend* think of it?'

'Oh, he loved it. How about your—companion?'

'She loved it too.' Which reply left Annabel still completely in the dark.

However, before she could frame a subtle, but probing question, Mr Strachan sailed up in the wake of the large flower-clad lady who had listened with such interest to Annabel's initial exchange with Drew in the hall. She turned out to be Mrs George Strachan. After the introductions, he forestalled any purely social chit-chat by reopening the research discussion. Fortified by Bob's excellent punch, Annabel won the first round hands down. Only momentarily outmanoeuvred, George Strachan finished his whisky and prepared to counter-attack. 'That's all very well——' he began masterfully.

His wife laid a restraining hand on his arm. 'I can see, if you can't, that you're getting nowhere, George. So why not leave it all to Drew? Miss Kerr is much more likely to yield to a handsome young man like him than to a crusty old bully like you!' And with that, she sailed away again, towing her silenced husband.

'I wonder,' said Drew, eyeing Annabel speculatively.

Annabel drank some more punch before taking up the challenge. 'And what exactly do you wonder?'

'Whether Maggie Strachan's faith in my persuasive powers is justified. After all, I haven't made much headway so far.'

'My mind is made up, Drew. I'll not be changing it.'

'You're talking about the research programme.'

'Of course. What else?'

'I wasn't,' he returned carefully, his eyes holding hers.

Could he *possibly* mean. . .? Best not to assume. 'You've lost me,' she said, not quite truthfully. 'Anyway, I thought that Mr Strachan was on call.'

'Now it's my turn to be perplexed,' returned Drew, with a look to match the words. 'However, to put you in the picture as they say—yes, this is his weekend on, but I'm standing in for him tonight. It wouldn't do to have the guest of honour absent, now would it?'

'I guess not. Is that why you were late, then?'

'I wasn't—I was early, but then I was called away by our over-zealous young houseman to deal with a simple bump on the head.' He sighed.

'Poor Michael! I do hope you didn't bawl him out too much. He's terrified of you, you know.'

'No, I didn't know.' Because of the press of people around the bar, they were now outside on the patio, there being nowhere else to go but out through the open french window. 'Is that what he told you?'

'He didn't need to. I can tell.'

'Amazing,' he said.

'What is?'

'The way you can pick up vibes from some folk, yet persistently fail to receive any of mine.'

At that, Annabel's heart gave such a deplorably unsophisticated little leap that she had to sit down on a convenient low stone wall to recover. 'Er—that must be because they're not exactly—consistent,' she observed, just to be going on with.

Drew sat down beside her, feet astride, elbows on thighs, his glass cradled in his hands. 'Neither are yours,' he said. 'So what are we going to do about it?'

'I suppose we could always try some plain——' she was saying, with a tiny thrill of excitement, when Bob looked out through the open window to interrupt apologetically.

'Sorry, Drew, but that's the hospital wanting you again.'

Drew got to his feet with a smothered imprecation that boded no good for Michael if it were he on the other end of that phone. 'Talks seem to have reached what politicians call the meaningful stage,' he reckoned, 'so don't go away, will you? I'll be back.'

Obediently, Annabel stayed where she was, but minutes later she heard a car hurrying away. Drew's expectations had been over-optimistic. Still, now at least she had a breathing space. She re-entered the house.

Bob was away from the bar now, and, apart from Bill Tait, deep in conversation with a pretty staff nurse from Outpatients, there was nobody else in the room whom she knew. She helped herself to more punch and edged through the crowd towards the door, meaning to find Jean and offer some help. What would Drew have said if he'd not been called away? Annabel knew what she'd have liked to hear, but she'd only been speaking the truth when she told him his signals were conflicting. Reproof, disapproval, nostalgic references to the past; they'd all been there. And to confuse things further, there was that gorgeous brunette. Jean probably knew all about her, but Annabel's pride wouldn't let her ask.

Jean, discovered in the kitchen, was looking more

frayed than Annabel had ever seen her. 'Bless you!' she breathed when Annabel appeared. 'I've definitely bitten off more than I can chew this time.' Bob appeared at that point and when he gave her an "I told you so" look, Jean added, 'Don't you dare! Anyway, you weren't supposed to hear that.'

'I'm quite sure I wasn't.' He gave his wife a hug and kissed the top of her dishevelled blonde mop. 'She's a wee marvel, my Jeannie,' he told Annabel, 'but it's taking her a gey long time to learn that she cannae do everything single-handed. Is there any more ice, sweetheart?'

'There is if you remembered to refill the ice trays,' retorted Bob's sweetheart crisply. 'Men!' she added fondly as he went out again. 'Now then—to work.'

Annabel had already noticed that the simple snacks Jean had originally planned had somehow grown into a full-scale buffet. 'I knew I shouldn't have taken yesterday off,' sighed Jean, following Annabel's glance. 'As you see, I got quite carried away. Still, as dear old Flossie Findhorn used to say to us at school, if a thing's worth doing at all, gels——'

'It's aye worth doing right,' finished Annabel on a chuckle.

But despite Jean's fears, she was actually quite well organised, and the girls soon had everything arranged in the dining-room. Jean surveyed the loaded table with some pride. 'Not so bad after all, and if you wouldn't mind cutting those quiches now, Annabel, I'll go and call them all to the trough.'

Hospital workers were renowned for their healthy appetites, and the call was promptly answered. For the next wee while, Jean and Annabel were constantly passing one another in the hall as they hurried to and fro, replenishing dishes. Annabel piled up a plate and put it on one side for Drew, because if he didn't return soon there'd be nothing left.

'Is that for me?' she heard in Jim Paul's lazy yet provocative drawl very close to her ear.

'Sorry,' she said. 'You're going to have to fend for yourself. This is for—absent friends.'

'Drew Maitland,' said Jim at once. 'I thought he had his eye on you, the crook dingo.'

Annabel had no idea what he meant by that, but felt sure it wasn't complimentary. 'I guess you'd say dog-in-the-manger, or so Lisa tells me.'

Was that a fact? Annabel hoped he was wrong. 'How is Lisa?' she asked. 'I haven't seen her tonight.'

'We had a bit of a row. She thinks she owns me on account of. . .' He shrugged expressively, tacitly telling Annabel exactly how things were, or had been, between them. 'So—I had to let her know she doesn't. So she stayed home, sulking.'

How defeatist! thought Annabel. She felt sorry for Lisa, but doubted if the girl's present course of action was the best way to handle a man like Jim. What he needed—and would soon be getting, if he didn't take his hand off her thigh pretty damn quick!—was a thorough put-down.

Annabel took the sleeve of his shirt between finger and thumb and lifted up the offending arm. Then she pushed a tablespoon into his hand. 'That's the best way I know of helping yourself to food,' she said briskly.

'That,' he returned, quite unabashed, 'rather depends on the kind of food a guy is after.' He had her hemmed in now, between the table end and the wall. And the hand was back, and creeping. Nothing for it but a direct reprimand. 'Frankly, I find your approach both crude and offensive,' Annabel retorted coolly. Then, because there was no other escape route, she dropped to her knees and dived under the table before Jim could stop her. She surfaced at the other end of the table, having banged her head twice and almost lost a shoe. 'Yes, can I help you?' she asked two startled guests who had obviously been searching for something, when she rose under their noses, more or less like Aphrodite from the foam.

It was salt they wanted, and, having found it for them among the desserts, where somebody had surprisingly put it, Annabel began to tidy up the table, which was now looking like the aftermath of a children's party.

'Splendid,' said Drew with warm approval next minute.

'I like to be useful,' returned Annabel, eyes firmly down to hide her pleasure at his reappearance.

He leaned across the table to explain, 'I was actually referring to the way you dealt with Jim Paul. I've never seen anything like it.'

'Extreme situations require extreme measures. Have you had any supper?'

'No, and neither, I suspect, have you. So how about collecting some supplies and going back to the garden?'

'What a good idea,' agreed Annabel with studied carelessness. But outside in the small paved garden, her confidence began to wane. Did she, after all, really want to pick up the threads of the past—always supposing that really was Drew's intention? He had dealt her one cruel blow. Was she willing to risk another? 'That call must have been another false alarm,' she supposed aloud to postpone the issue.

'Not entirely.' He didn't elaborate, but scooped up a forkful of salad and chewed thoughtfully for a few minutes. 'This is some spread Jean has put on,' he remarked then.

'It certainly is. But then she does everything so well.'

'Indeed she does. Did you know she decorated the sitting-room herself?'

'No, I didn't. And with all that difficult cornice-work too. . .'

'Precisely. You know what we're doing, don't you?'

'Having supper?'

'Skirmishing. We both know fine that we came out here to continue an interrupted conversation.'

'Oh!'

'You were in the middle of saying something when I was called away,' prompted Drew.

'Was I? I—don't remember what.'

'I do. Your exact words were "We could always try some plain"—and then we were interrupted. I can only think you meant some plain speaking.'

'I suppose I must have.'

'But you're not now, are you?'

'Not what?'

'Speaking plainly. No, you're backing off again. What are you afraid of, Annabel?'

'I don't think I'm afraid of anything.'

'Then why are you so reluctant to discuss exactly where it is we're at?'

Annabel put down her plate, the food hardly touched. 'If I am, it must be because I honestly don't know.'

'But is that not just what we're trying to establish?'

'I—I guess so.'

'One point of agreement after much shilly-shallying, then. So let's try something else. Do you still hate me?' queried Drew.

'Don't be silly! Anyway, I never did.'

'Good. Because I stopped feeling bitter towards you a long, long time ago.'

'Bitter? I don't understand,' said Annabel. 'Why should you have felt bitter towards me?'

'Because you didn't answer my letters,' he told her.

'Really? Somehow, I never expected you to feel like that. It seemed—well, best to make a complete break.'

'Having decided that you didn't really love me after all.'

'No—because I knew that I did. I couldn't have coped with—with half measures.'

'And now?' asked Drew.

'Now I know that most of life is compromise.'

'What I really meant is how do you feel about me now?'

'I—don't know. Anyway, why should I tell you when I've no idea how you feel about me?' Annabel wanted to know.

'I'd have thought that was obvious. Anyway, the plain speaking was your idea.'

So it had been—but what was obvious? His reason for getting her to speak first, or the way he felt about her now? After a moment's thought, she said carefully, 'This could go on all night, so let me see. How *do* I feel? I think I quite like you as a man and I certainly admire you enormously as a surgeon. Will that do?'

'For a start.'

Did he really expect her to let him away with that? 'You don't want much, do you? Now it's your turn to be frank.'

Drew had come so close that their bodies were almost touching. 'You've changed,' he said softly. 'You've learned a lot about life and about men too. I'm confessing now that I find the new Annabel even more attractive than the old one.' He put his hands on her shoulders and pulled her unhurriedly towards him.

At the instant their lips met, it was as if the intervening years had never been. But they had—and Annabel couldn't forget. Somehow she had got to keep her head.

She returned his kiss, but when they drew apart she murmured, 'Nice—yes, very nice. You've learned a lot too, but I'm not aiming to get carried away.'

There was a slight increase in the pressure of his hands on her shoulders before Drew said, 'All right, then let's take it a day at a time. . .'

'No strings and no expectations——' How ironic! That had been *his* stipulation last time.

'And leave the rest to fate?'

'I'm sure that's best,' agreed Annabel breathlessly, just before his mouth found hers again.

It was the noise and bustle of the first departures that broke the spell. Annabel sprang away from Drew, straightening her dress and patting her shining bob.

He thrust his hands in his pockets and leaned against the corner of the house, watching her. 'Perhaps you're not that much changed after all,' he said.

'What do you mean?'

'All this unsophisticated alarm. What are you afraid of now?'

'Somebody might have seen us.'

'So what? Somebody will have noticed us coming out here, and they'll not have supposed we came out to discuss the weather.'

'I don't want people talking,' said Annabel.

'They'll talk if they want to, and there's no way of stopping that. The thing to do is to agree with everything that's said and add a few obviously ridiculous details of your own.'

'It sounds to me as if you've had a lot of experience in managing this sort of thing,' observed Annabel crisply.

'I've had my share. And so, no doubt, have you.'

She couldn't deny that, but somehow her experience was acceptable, because she knew there'd never been anything serious in it. Drew's experience, she felt, was quite another matter. 'I think I ought to be going soon,' she said.

'Me too. I want to take another look at the patient I admitted earlier. Are you free on Tuesday evening?'

'Probably, but I'll need to check at home.' And why Tuesday? Why not tomorrow?

As though reading her thoughts, Drew said, 'Tomorrow would have been nicer, but then I am on call. Officially.' He came up to Annabel again and clasped her slim waist. 'That little inn on the road to Alford—remember? We could dine there and see if it's changed as much as we think we have.'

'No!' Very definitely Annabel did not want to re-tread old ground. That would be dangerous; too evocative. 'Would you mind if we went somewhere different—somewhere we've never been before?'

'Of course, if that's what you want.' Drew seemed rather surprised; definitely not worried, then, as she had been, about the possibility of awakening old feelings. Were his memories less precious than hers? Yet he had remembered the inn. . .

'Yes—thank you,' she murmured.

He answered that with a brief hug and an even briefer kiss before letting her go. 'You go back into the sitting-room, and I'll go in by the front door. Will that be discreet enough for you?'

'Don't put it all on me!' she riposted with a small, nicely judged laugh. 'You've got an image to take care of too.' But why should she have visualised that radiant brunette beauty while saying that?

Drew laughed too. 'Somehow, I don't see you damaging anybody's prospects. Quite the contrary.'

'You have changed after all,' Annabel considered

thoughtfully, having chosen her moment for returning unobserved to the house.

She stayed on when all the other guests had gone, in order to help Jean and Bob with the tidying up. To her intense relief, neither of them so much as hinted at the time she'd spent outside alone with Drew. Annabel had quite a lot of personal adjusting to do before dealing with outsider interest!

She drove home in a happy daze. On his own admission, Drew still found her as attractive—correction, more attractive than he had when they first met. So his acid comments about Adam, Jim and Michael could be put down to jealousy and not disapproval, as she had tried to make herself believe. And the brunette? She couldn't be as important as her own jealousy—oh, yes, she'd certainly been jealous—had led Annabel to believe. A good friend—a long-standing friend, but nothing more. Otherwise, why was Drew apparently ready to try again with her?

She would be sensible, though; she would let him set the pace. There must be none of that mindless plunging over the cliff that had been so disastrous last time.

Mrs Kerr had gone to bed by the time Annabel reached home, but she had left a note on the hall table. Gran was as good as gold all evening and then went to bed without a murmur, it ran.

What a contrast to the stress and drama earlier that day! Annabel's full lips twisted in a little smile. Her mother was obviously much better at handling Gran than she. So was it possible that she had over-reacted that morning, thus exacerbating her grandmother's volatility? Perhaps Gran wasn't so seriously ill after all.

CHAPTER SEVEN

WHEN Annabel arrived at the hospital next morning, Drew was parking his car. He had seen her and strode eagerly across to open the car door for her. 'Annabel! Did I dream it, or have we really got a date for tomorrow night?' he asked, smiling into her eyes.

'If you were dreaming, then so was I,' she answered lightly. 'Of course, there may have been something hallucinatory in the food. . .'

'Not so. Neither of us ate enough of it.'

'True. Besides, nobody else seemed to be affected.'

'I'd not have noticed if they had been,' Drew returned softly. 'I was far too preoccupied with you.'

While others had parked and gone, they were still standing there with the open door between them. Annabel pulled at it. 'People are going to wonder why we're still here.'

'You're paranoid!' chuckled Drew, but he stood back obediently.

'No, just discreet,' insisted Annabel, locking her car. 'I know only too well what a hotbed of gossip a hospital can be.'

'How come?' Drew pulled a ferocious face. 'No, don't tell me—you're only trying to make me jealous.'

'But of course,' she laughed. 'How clever of you to guess.' She looked at the clock high up in the central tower of the ornate Victorian building. 'We were early five minutes ago. Soon——'

'Race you to the wards, then.'

'Be your age!' she advised on a chuckle. 'Consultants don't run except in emergency.'

'Sorry. It must be because I'm feeling twenty-four again. Oh, hell!' Mr Strachan had parked quite near them and now he was signalling across the divide. 'See you later, then,' Drew whispered, before joining his colleague.

Annabel went on her way smiling. Why had she been feeling scared? This thing was going to be a doddle.

Jean wouldn't be in until twelve today—she was working the late shift to give herself time to recover from her party—so Annabel got her Monday morning update from Michael instead.

Michael had had a heavy weekend and he looked exhausted. 'Casualty calls mostly,' he explained on a stifled yawn. 'Our own patients were very well behaved.'

'But there was one admission,' prompted Annabel.

'Now how did you——? Of course, Sister's party. I had to call Mr Maitland away from it twice.' Michael looked downcast at the memory. 'Anyway, just as a precaution he admitted the second chap. But I think he'll be going home today.'

'So we're more or less as we were, then, are we?'

'One of last Wednesday's patients for stereotaxis has been having severe headaches and Nurse Kirk has been in quite a lot of pain again. Otherwise, yes.'

'Thanks, Michael. I'll get to it, then.'

'And I'd better do the same. Annabel, I was going to ask you if you'd like to go to the cinema or something tonight, but. . .'

'But you'd probably fall asleep in the middle of the film, by the look of you. I think you'd be better to get an early night, m'lad,' she was advising him when the two consultants entered.

George Strachan shot her a look which contrived to

be both approving and dismissive, and, after exchanging amused glances with Drew, she faded quietly out of the office.

Donnie was not as stiff as Annabel had feared he might be after getting less intensive treatment over the weekend. Colin was positively co-operative and Seonaid quite chatty in a jerky voice she'd not quite regained control of. Claire was full of her Saturday at home and Christine was still sulking at being excluded. 'Never mind, you'll be getting home to stay any day now,' Annabel pointed out encouragingly before she and Claire set out for Claire's morning walk. Today they were also going to tackle the stairs. Everybody improving, thank goodness.

Well, almost everybody. As Michael had told her, Nurse Kirk was still having a lot of pain and was naturally rather downcast. Tactful questioning elicited fears of not being able to return to the job with old people that she loved, and Annabel suspected that anxiety was playing a part in her symptoms. The consultants and the registrar would be in Outpatients all morning, so a word with Jean when she came on at noon, then. . .

As usual, the morning flew by at the speed of light. Was it imagination, or did the time really pass more slowly in the lecture-room? Annabel reflected again on the relative peace of teaching, as compared with the bustle of the wards, where she must always be ready to depart from routine.

There followed a rushed canteen lunch with Miss Tannoch, who was way up to high doh, because two of the juniors had given notice. Annabel successfully dissuaded her from consoling herself with apple crumble—far too much topping—and thick hospital custard. 'How about a peach, Miss Tannoch? So much less sleep-making before a busy afternoon.' They were keeping up the pretence that Annabel didn't know about Miss Tannoch's diabetes.

A simply splendid session in the gym that afternoon, with Mrs Plockton in great form and only nearly falling over once, Mr Cairns and Danny enjoying her gaiety as usual and Danny much more cheerful after his weekend at home. See you later, Drew had said when they met that morning, but Annabel had to go off duty without another meeting.

Annabel drove to work next morning in a curiously mixed mood of depression and elation. Gran had been so difficult last night. She had quarrelled repeatedly with Agnes, causing Agnes to take offence and leave early. But to balance the unhappy state of affairs at home there was this evening's date with Drew to look forward to. 'Just going for an evening out with a colleague,' she had explained casually to her mother when Mrs Kerr wondered aloud why Annabel was wearing her good green Country Casuals.

Mrs Kerr then obligingly assumed that Annabel meant one of the physios, and Annabel left it at that. Time enough to tell her that Drew was back when she could see where it all was leading—if anywhere.

Another emergency had been admitted the night before. 'Girl of nineteen in a road traffic accident. Moderate concussion/contusion injury,' Jean explained succinctly. 'The boyfriend, who had been drinking, got off scot-free at the wheel—I'm telling you, Annabel, there's nae justice. Anyway, usual routine of chest care and passive movement. How did you find Ian Buckie yesterday?'

'Fine—relatively speaking. Of course, I can't let him

do much for fear of displacement, but I'm pretty sure his muscle power is holding up.'

'Good. Drew will be relieved. I know he's been wondering if he should have operated and applied internal fixation. And talking of Drew. . .'

'Yes, did you remember to ask him about Nurse Kirk's increased pain?' asked Annabel quickly, before Jean could make a more personal comment as intuition warned she was about to do.

Jean signalled awareness of the dodge with one arched eyebrow. 'I did, and he has changed her analgesic. She's much more comfortable now.'

'Oh, good. Then if there's nothing else. . .?'

'No, that's all. About the patients,' returned Jean.

'Thanks very much, then, Jean dear.' Annabel beat a hasty retreat. It wasn't nice, choking off a friend like that, but she wasn't ready to discuss Drew yet.

Today took even longer to pass than yesterday. Was that because Annabel was eager for the evening? But at last she was free to dash down to Physio to join the queue for the shower. Half the staff seemed to be going out straight from work today.

It was very hot, so Annabel left off her jacket, carrying it casually over one shoulder by a finger hooked through the loop. Again she'd not seen Drew all day, and there was relief mixed in with the little surge of excitement that overtook her at the sight of him waiting by the silver Volvo. Absurd, really, to have wondered if he'd been keeping out of her way because he regretted his invitation, but there it was. She had.

She was further reassured by the way Drew drank in her appearance with such obvious pleasure. 'That green—with your hair. . .' He gave a long low whistle before settling her in the car.

Annabel watched him walk round: deeply tanned,

casual, yet athletic-looking, in pale trousers and a matching shirt open at the neck. 'You're not looking so bad yourself,' she conceded as they set off. 'So where are we going?'

'As per instructions, somewhere we've never been before. Together, that is.'

Was he allowing that she might have been with somebody else, or telling her that he had? No matter. 'All right, be like that,' she retorted carelessly. 'I don't care as long as the food's good.'

'You always did like your nosh,' laughed Drew. 'Not that it shows,' he added after a lightning sidelong appraisal of her neat figure in trim straight skirt and sleeveless patterned top.

'Oh, what a relief! Though surely it's a bit early for the dreaded middle-aged spread to descend, is it not?'

'Stranger things have happened. I'm remembering a poor lass I saw some years back. A pituitary tumour had precipitated her into the menopause in her late twenties. Fortunately the boss was able to remove it successfully, after which she gradually reverted to her former attractive self. Annabel, why the devil are we talking shop?'

'Because it's the only thing we've got in common—or because it's your favourite subject?'

After another quick glance he corrected, 'Second favourite.' They had reached the end of the High Street now and he turned off on to the road that would eventually take them up Deeside.

'Would it be indelicate of me to ask what is your first?' asked Annabel.

'No, just typically feminine. Don't forget that curiosity is supposed to have killed some cat or other.'

He pretended to shrink in terror from her playfully threatened backhander. 'Please do not attack the driver unless you want to end up in hospital,' he intoned, before asking with palpable offhandedness, 'What have you been doing with yourself all these years, Annabel?'

So he wasn't going to tell her. 'Three years in Glasgow and five in London. I thought I'd told you that.'

'I didn't ask where, I asked what.'

The houses were fewer and further apart now. Soon they would be heading west on a winding, tree-lined road.

'Being a physio, of course.'

Drew gave an exasperated sigh. 'Can you not help it, or are you being deliberately maddening? Surely you must realise that what I want to know is if there was ever anybody else? A *man*!' he added to give her no more chances for evasion.

'Quite a few, actually,' she told him.

'And does that mean you're hard to please or easily bored?'

'I like to think it means I'm rather attractive.'

'Never mind the mock modesty—you know damn well you are!' A pause long enough for Annabel to relish that. 'But—nobody you thought of marrying, for instance?'

'I wouldn't say that.' No, indeed not! She'd *thought* about it—only she'd never managed to bring herself to the point. 'After all, marriage is a very serious step.'

'And you never met anybody you wanted to marry!'

He had said that a shade too confidently. 'I wouldn't say that either.'

'Then what the blazes would you say?' He was visibly nettled now.

'Just that my—my earliest experiences taught me the value of looking before I leap.'

'He who hesitates is lost,' stated Drew flatly.

'My goodness, somebody has changed his tune!'

Annabel murmured as Drew slowed the car before turning right into a narrow road that would take them down to the river.

Either he didn't hear that, or he wasn't prepared to pick up the challenge. The next time he spoke it was to comment on the variety of birdlife in the woods on either side of the road.

Infuriating so-and-so! Annabel was thinking as they emerged into a gravelled car park that was almost full. So soon? But glancing at the dashboard clock she discovered that their journey had taken three-quarters of an hour.

This place had once been a mill, as evidenced by the great wheel on the riverside wall. The whole place had been expertly restored. 'You've not been here before,' guessed Drew, noting her interest.

'No, I've not, and I'm bound to say it looks very special.' Through sparkling, small-paned windows, she could see tables dressed all in green, each with flowers and a lighted candle.

'It is—or so I'm told.' So he'd not been here before either. The place was new to both of them; a new beginning. . .

The last person Annabel had expected to see there, propping up the bar with several other prosperous-looking farming types was Adam Keith. 'Damn!' she muttered, stopping dead in the doorway so that Drew bumped into her.

Over her head, he followed her glance and remarked through tightened lips, 'This must be a regular hazard for a girl of your wide—acquaintance.'

'He's going to mind so much,' was Annabel's honest but unguarded reaction.

'Are you suggesting that I would not?'

'Adam doesn't have your sophistication.'

'I'm not sure I like the implication.'

What was happening to this evening that was meant to be so wonderful? If only she'd not been so evasive and difficult on the way here! 'I suppose we could always——' she began placatingly.

'Bolt? Not necessary. Your unsophisticated friend and his pals are being led away to the grill-room, and as we're booked into the main restaurant your sins will not be coming home to roost on this occasion.'

'I thought you hadn't been here before?' she queried.

'I haven't, but I did take care to find out all about it first.' Now that Adam and his friends had disappeared, Drew propelled Annabel towards the bar. 'What would you like to drink?'

A treble Scotch to calm my jangled nerves. . .'A small dry sherry, please.'

'You've graduated from the sweet stuff, then,' observed Drew, having ordered two dry sherries.

How very grown up she had felt the first time Drew took her out for a meal and she asked for a sweet sherry as an aperitif. And he had remembered too. 'Now I have a more educated palate.' She smiled at him, but he didn't smile back.

'Achieved, no doubt, with the aid of all those men— past and present.'

Annabel disdained to reply and they sipped their sherry in silence. She was feeling vaguely resentful. Was that because Drew, while determined to find out all he could about her past, had told her nothing of his own? 'How long did you stay at the Royal that first time, Drew?' she asked.

Roused from apparent rapt contemplation of all the bottles lined up behind the bar, Drew turned his head sharply. 'Eh? You mean—two years.' He pushed their glasses towards the barman for a refill.

Very informative that had been! 'And then?'

'A year at the General, one in the States and four in Edinburgh. Then back here to the Royal two months ago.'

'Picking up your Fellowship somewhere along the way?'

'Plus a Master's. It's necessary to be well qualified these days, with all the competition.'

'All that study'll not have left you much time for relaxation.'

'It didn't.'

'And yet you don't seem to be—out of practice.' He knows perfectly well what I'm driving at, Annabel realised, watching a tiny smile playing around his lean, humorous mouth.

'Oh, I practised hard as well as imbibing all the theory. My seniors made sure of that.'

'Now who's being deliberately evasive?' challenged Annabel.

At first she thought he meant to keep it up, and then with a shrug, he said, 'There were girls—I'm not monkish. But there was never anybody who stood out from the crowd.'

Not even that brunette? wondered Annabel, as the waiter came to tell them that their table was ready. 'It seems to me that you're the one who's hard to please and easily bored,' she observed lightly as they made their way to the dining-room.

'I'm not bored now,' Drew insisted. 'Or rather, I'll not be if we can get off our pasts and concentrate on enjoying the present.'

He was quite right, of course; even though it was he who had begun it. Raking up the past was morbid. Annabel regarded her generous plateful of smoked salmon and observed thoughtfully, 'This looks like a splendid way to start enjoying the present.'

'You don't think my company might have something to contribute?'

'That's very possible, but I wasn't going to say so in case you got above yourself.'

Drew chuckled appreciatively. 'Not much chance of that, with you in such cracking form!'

'You're not exactly short on form yourself.'

They were back to the light and easy exchanges they had shared so briefly during that meeting in the car park yesterday. If only we could keep it like this, Annabel wished.

It lasted until they were leaving and came face to face with Adam in the car park. He looked from Annabel to Drew and back as if he could hardly believe his eyes. 'Good evening, Annabel,' he said at last in a voice that was stiff with displeasure.

'H-hello, Adam.' Nothing for it but a bold face. 'Drew, I want you to meet my old friend Adam Keith.' No, she didn't, and Adam wasn't really an old friend in either sense. 'Adam, this is a colleague of mine, Drew Maitland.' That was true—as far as it went.

Muttered how-do-you-dos and no handshake. The air was electric.

'I certainly never expected to see you here tonight, Adam,' Annabel tossed inanely into the heavy silence.

'I'm quite sure you didn't,' returned Adam, pouncing on the chance she had set up for him. 'Well, I'll not detain you; you'll likely have things to discuss with your colleague.' The way he had pronounced it, 'colleague' was a dirty word.

'He's jealous,' observed Drew superfluously as they watched Adam stamp heavily across the car park and throw himself into his Audi. As he drove away, they had to step back quickly to avoid being peppered with gravel.

'He's hurt—I knew he would be! And I wish I could be sure he'll not mention this at home,' Annabel added, half to herself. The last thing she wanted was her mother told, with all the questions that would bring.

'Playing a double game, then, are we?' Drew asked acidly.

'There's such a thing as discretion,' she retaliated.

'Would that be the "in" word for deceit?'

'All right—so I didn't say who I was going out with tonight. What's so significant about that?' she demanded.

'That depends,' he shrugged.

'On what?'

'On *why* you didn't say.'

'I didn't say because it would have led to questions.'

'Such as?' Drew wanted to know.

'Why on earth I was being such a fool as to take up with you again, maybe!' hissed Annabel, her control going.

'Somehow, I can't imagine your sensible mother asking such a loaded question. But tell me honestly, Annabel. Is it the question or the answer that troubles you?'

That cooled her down. He had gone straight to the core of the problem. 'I just don't—don't fancy life getting any more complicated than it is already.'

'Nobody could quarrel with that,' Drew considered quietly. 'But you haven't answered my question.'

'How can I, when I don't know the answer?' she asked forlornly, defences temporarily demolished.

Drew took her hand and Annabel let him lead her into a screen of birch and rowan trees between the mill and the river. Unresisting, she let him fold her in his arms. And when he kissed her, she kissed him back, conscious only of the undiminished strength of his attraction for her. She could have told him the answer now. Of course she was afraid! He'd tired of her once; so why not twice? And if he did—could she bear it?

Drew sensed her withdrawal. 'What's wrong now?' he sighed against her cheek.

'I—I said I didn't fancy life getting more complicated.'

'Sorry, I thought I was simplifying things by getting down to the central issue.'

'You're rushing me,' she prevaricated. 'This is only a first date, remember.' What had possessed her? That was a perfectly ridiculous thing to say!

Drew pulled away and stared down at her in amazement. 'I don't believe what I'm hearing. You sound like some wilting nineteenth-century miss. Anyway, it isn't the first, is it? Not by a long way.'

Which was the trouble, of course. It was the past and its agonising ending that was distorting the present. It was easy to decide on forgetting. Much, much harder to succeed. Why on earth couldn't she have kept up the detached response she'd achieved in Jean's garden? 'It was seeing Adam,' she said. It wasn't, but that would do. 'Things were all right until then. I'm really sorry, Drew. I'd wanted this to be a happy evening.'

'Cheer up,' he said bracingly. 'It's not been all bad. Let's resolve to do better next time, shall we?'

'Nothing really bothers you, does it, Drew?' she asked with mixed feelings of envy and regret.

Drew emitted a brief gust of astonished laughter. 'We can hardly do worse, if that's how I'm coming across. Annabel, you're priceless!'

'I thought I was only being honest.' She paused. 'Seems we're giving out conflicting signals again.'

'Then cracking the code had better get top priority,' he returned firmly, putting an arm around her slim waist for the walk back to the car.

Drew took charge of the conversation on the return journey; general subjects only, interspersed with amusing tales of encounters with difficult patients in which he had always come off worst. He never did mind telling stories against himself, remembered Annabel, wiping away tears of laughter after one such. If only she could forget the painful past and try again as Drew seemed willing to do. . .

She forgot all right when it came time to say goodnight. The strength and power of his kisses then blotted out all but the exciting and blissful present.

'Lovely, delicious Annabel,' he murmured afterwards against her quivering mouth. 'Just as beguiling as ever!'

Not beguiling enough, though. At least, not at eighteen, she wasn't. Keep the heid, lassie. . . Annabel pulled out of his arms and pushed a hand through her rumpled hair. 'Are you sure you don't have any Irish blood, Drew Maitland?' she asked lightly. 'Because you surely know how to lay on the blarney!'

A moment's silence, then Drew remarked quietly, 'I only wish I had. It seems to me that a man needs more blarney than I can muster to get through to you now. Come on, I'll walk you to your car.'

CHAPTER EIGHT

WHEN Annabel left the hospital next evening, Drew was still there. She knew that because she saw him through the window of his consulting-room. He was bent over his desk, concentration in every line. Today was ops day and he had been in theatre for most of it; probably without giving her a thought. Whereas Annabel had had the utmost difficulty in keeping her mind on her work. She'd been tired too, not having slept much after an evening of such mingled pleasure, conflict and uncertainty. Perhaps it was as well that she and Drew hadn't met that day; a breathing space would be good for them both. And she had actually thought this was all going to be a doddle!

When nearly home, Annabel turned her attention to her other problem. How would Gran be tonight?

Her mother had obviously been crying, though two minutes with Gran, lucid and tranquil, convinced Annabel that it couldn't have been on her account.

Annabel was wrong. 'Mid-morning,' said Mrs Kerr when she and her daughter were shut in the kitchen, safely out of earshot. 'She was quite all right when I gave her her coffee, then the very next minute—this queer noise, staring eyes, coffee all down her front and the cup on the floor. . .' Mrs Kerr caught her breath on a sob.

Oh, lord—another fit! Two in four days. This was not the usual pattern of senile dementia. 'Mother—?'

'I phoned the surgery as soon as I'd got her settled,'

continued Mrs Kerr, anticipating Annabel's next question. 'And young Dr Faulds came round within the hour.'

'And he suggested a specialist.'

'No, he didn't. By then Gran was as right as a trivet and at her most gracious. She even knew what time it was for once, because she invited him to lunch! He thinks I'm over-anxious, Annabel—he thinks I exaggerated. He—he suggested putting me on tranquillisers. Me! They've none of them ever caught her in one of her moods—not once.' Poor Mrs Kerr began to cry again.

Annabel put her arms around her mother. 'Listen, darling, I'm going to have a word with the neurosurgeons at the hospital about this. It can't do any harm, and they might be able to suggest something. I'm sure we can manage it without offending the doctors here.' And even if they couldn't, Annabel would still go ahead, because Gran obviously needed treatment and her mother couldn't take much more of this.

But their GP couldn't be blamed, and neither could that psychiatrist. Neither of them could be expected to act on hearsay alone. If they did, it would be far too easy for families to banish their awkward, elderly members.

Acute observation of her grandmother all through supper failed to show Annabel any sign of anything other than the occasional lapse of concentration common to so many in Gran's age group. And Annabel's surveillance didn't go unnoticed. 'Have I got a smut on my nose, miss?' the old lady eventually demanded.

'Why, no, Gran——'

'Then don't stare! It's very rude.'

'Sorry, Gran.'

* * *

Right after the supper dishes were washed and put away, Annabel had a phone call. 'Annabel? About tomorrow. I'm afraid I—I can't make it.'

'I'm very sorry, Adam.' Annabel wasn't sure whether she was expressing regret at their cancelled date, or apologising for last night's unfortunate meeting.

'Yes, well—something's come up.'

'I quite understand.' Annabel knew exactly what that something was. 'Another time, perhaps?'

'I'll give that some thought.'

'Thank you, Adam.'

There was a pause during which Annabel was expecting him to ring off. Instead he asked, 'How are things at Rowan House today?'

'Not good, I'm afraid. Gran had another fit this morning.'

'Perhaps that colleague of yours can suggest something. Brains are his line, are they not?'

Now how did he know that? Had he been looking Drew up in the Medical Directory? 'That's right—and I've already discussed Gran with him. Briefly.'

'Yes, you will have. I have to go now—Mother's calling. Goodbye, Annabel.'

'Goodnight, Adam. And thanks for letting me know.'

Her answer was a metallic click as Adam replaced the receiver. He was almost certainly suffering from an attack of hurt pride. In any other man, Annabel would have suspected a degree of childishness as well. But, having got to know Adam rather better lately, she realised that he wasn't to be compared with other men. Living always in his mother's strong shadow, Adam had never really had the chance to mature.

Before she could pursue that train of thought any further, the phone rang again. 'Annabel? It's Drew.'

A rush of exhilaration, followed by a tiny pause,

during which Annabel schooled herself to say calmly, 'Oh, hello. Are you still at the hospital?'

'I am. I've been going over some of Lisa's latest findings, but somehow I can't seem to concentrate.'

'I thought you could always concentrate on work.'

'So did I.' He sounded both sorry and surprised about that.

'Are you on call?' she asked.

'Yes, but so far all is quiet. Weekends are usually the worst.' Another pause. 'Actually, I'm on this coming one—which only leaves tomorrow night.'

Another chance? Could be. Don't mess it up. . . 'And naturally you want to put it to the best possible use.'

'How very understanding you can be when you try,' he considered in a teasing voice.

'Glad you noticed. So what are you planning for that night of freedom?'

'What I would really like to do tomorrow,' Drew began in a confidential way, 'is to spend the evening with an old flame I was once—extremely fond of.'

'Then I do hope you manage it. Anything I can do to help?'

'I think you know the answer to that one,' he returned firmly. 'Shall we discuss the details tomorrow?'

'Why not now?'

'Because tonight I have to work on my blarney,' he explained with that throaty chuckle she never could resist.

'Please don't work too hard at it—it wouldn't be fair to a girl!' she teased.

'Thanks for the clue, my angel. Now of course I shall burn the midnight oil.'

'You—you——'

'Is this a private call?' interrupted the hospital telephone operator with brisk efficiency before Annabel had come up with a suitable description.

'Keep your husband warm and give him plenty of hot sweet tea, Mrs McGonigal,' said Drew with tremendous presence of mind, before wishing her goodnight and hanging up on her helpless shriek of laughter. She felt wonderfully, gloriously alive now. Was everything going to turn out happily after all?

Although purposely starting work early next morning, Annabel only just had time to treat her chesty patients before Mr Strachan came steaming on to the wards. A nurse was sent round to summon the stragglers, and Jean whispered as Annabel joined the retinue, 'Something tells me this round is going to be one to remember!'

'You were saying, Sister?'

'Just good morning to Miss Kerr, sir,' Jean answered calmly. She and Drew were the only ones not in awe of the senior surgeon.

'Very polite of you, but we have a lot to get through this morning. Come along—come along!'

Short of breaking into a canter, which would have been both undignified and difficult with the heavy trolley of case-notes and X-rays to push, they couldn't have made any more speed. Jean had read his mood aright.

They started as usual in the RHI ward, where Donnie Helm was found to be very restless and muttering to himself. 'You've certainly wrought a change with your cryotherapy, Miss Kerr,' observed the boss. 'I hope it's a useful one. What do you think, Drew?'

'No question. His conscious level is markedly up and he's responding to all kinds of stimuli.'

'Splendid. You'll be closing off his tracheostomy soon, no doubt. Where is Colin Montrose, Sister?'

'Transferred to Orthopaedics yesterday, sir.'

'But we still have this unfortunate young lassie to take care of,' said Mr Strachan, bending over the inert form of Lesley Cochrane, admitted after the car crash on Monday evening.

'I can't detect any change here, Drew. Can you?'

'No, but at least she's no worse. Her chest is clear, her muscle tone only minimally raised, and she is responding to painful stimuli.'

'Her skin is perfectly all right too, sir,' Jean put in before he could cast a slur on her nurses and their skills.

'In three days? So I should hope, my good girl. And the boyfriend got off scot-free, did he?'

'Just a few scratches and bruises, but I understand there's to be a prosecution for driving while under the influence of alcohol, and it's expected that he'll lose his licence,' reported Drew.

'If I had my way, such irresponsible hooligans'd lose their balls,' said the boss, not mincing matters.

'The boy is genuinely upset about Lesley, sir,' offered Bill Tait when the suppressed titters had died away.

'So he should be,' was the crisp reply. Mr Strachan stroked the girl's white forehead with a gentle hand. 'What a pity you had to suffer to bring him to his senses. Ah well, let's hope he's learned his lesson.' He swung round to Annabel. 'Now then. How is Seonaid getting on?'

'She's got a surprise for you this morning, sir, but I'm not allowed to tell you what it is.'

'Come along then—come along. Don't keep me in suspense.' He shooed them all out into the corridor and along to the women's ward.

Seonaid was poised ready for action, and the second the surgeons appeared in the doorway, she hoisted herself unsteadily to her feet and stood there, feet wide apart but quite unsupported for several seconds, before beginning to shake and collapsing back into her chair.

All the praise she got brought on a spasm of giggles which led to a coughing fit, and it was Mr Strachan himself who poured out the reviving glass of water. He could on occasion be quite impossible! Nevertheless, Annabel could see why everybody from Drew downwards thought so much of the man.

On they went. Christine was discharged and a five-day week for Claire decided upon. For Mrs Plockton and Danny McMahon as well; Mr Strachan was a firm believer in weekends at home to revive the flagging morale of patients obliged to spend long periods in hospital. Mr Cairns could also have gone on the list, but he had no relatives living near enough to take him.

This provoked another of Mr Strachan's dissertations on the undesirability of modern life and the scattering of families, which left so many old folk alone and unsupported. They all kept silent. Putting forward an alternative view would have been useless, when the boss didn't admit another interpretation of his particular hobbyhorse. 'He should have been a geriatrician,' Michael murmured daringly to Annabel as they moved on.

Ian Buckie was next; as well as could be expected, but somewhat depressed at the prospect of his long haul back to normality. Drew had been expecting a reaction of this sort, and he promised to return for a chat later that day.

The backs next, with the usual ratio of discharges to new patients after yesterday's theatre list. Nurse Kirk was happy with her new pain reliever, but one of the new backs was another nurse with a slipped disc. 'An occupational hazard,' underlined Mr Strachan with a heavy sigh. 'Can you physios not teach these poor girls to work in pairs when lifting patients, Miss Kerr?'

'We do, sir—it's part of preliminary nurse training—but when they're short-staffed and it's a matter of the patient's comfort or her own well-being, there seems to be only one choice for a born nurse.'

Being unable to find an instant comment on that, Mr Strachan demanded instead, 'Did you do assessments on last week's Parkinsonian patients as I asked?'

'Yes, sir. You'll find them in the case-notes.'

'I trust you mean your findings and not the patients.'

Annabel coloured faintly, but declined to confirm so absurd a premise.

'I like clear and unequivocal answers to my questions, Miss Kerr.'

'Yes, sir.' A picture of his large, commanding wife came to mind, and Annabel forgave him. He needed to flex his muscles somewhere, for he wasn't top dog at home, that was for sure!

As the procession wound its way back to Jean's office for coffee and discussion, Annabel mentally braced herself for another attempt to overturn her decision not to take part in research. Sure enough it came, once the problems arising from the round had been dealt with.

'With Mrs Craig ill, you'll be behind schedule with the project, Drew,' Mr Strachan began cunningly.

'Yes, we are a bit, but it can't be helped.'

'And with Barbara Craig likely to be off sick for another six weeks. . .' George Strachan fixed Annabel with his famous stare.

'So I heard, sir, and I'm just hoping that I'll not be obliged to hand in my notice before she returns,' Annabel returned firmly.

'What's this? Are you threatening me, Miss Kerr?'

'Indeed not, sir. Just expressing an unfortunate possibility. Things at home——'

'Surely it doesn't take two of you to manage one mildly confused old lady?'

'Probably not, but one with lightning mood changes, violent outbursts of aggression and frequent petit mal fits is quite a handful.'

There were gasps all round, and Mr Strachan asked urgently 'What do her doctors say?'

'Her GP has never seen her anything but lucid and he's inclined to think that my mother is over-reacting. And my grandmother was also quite lucid when she was seen by a psychiatrist.'

'No scan? No investigations?'

'None, sir.'

'Sit down, Miss Kerr, and think very carefully before you answer any of the questions I'm going to put to you.'

Ten minutes later, he said, 'Bring your grandmother to see me tomorrow at one. My outpatient clinic should be over by then.'

'Oh, thank you, sir! I can't tell you how much I appreciate this.'

'Then don't try. In any case, actions speak louder than words, as I shall probably remind you if I manage to sort out your grandmother's problem.'

Annabel understood perfectly. 'If you do, sir, I shall be only too happy to stand in for Mrs Craig.'

'I hope you all heard that,' said Mr Strachan. 'Now then, Drew. I've got a patient to see at the General before lunch, and I'd value your opinion of him if you've got time to come with me.'

'I'll make the time.' Drew was not the one to miss the prospect of being in on an interesting case. But he hadn't forgotten Annabel. With a barely perceptible

wink, he said, 'There's something I must discuss with
you some time today, Miss Kerr. Could you spare me
ten minutes about four?'

'Of course, Mr Maitland.'

'Thank you. Well, if Sister doesn't need me, I'm all
yours, George.'

The two consultants went off deep in discussion and
the rest of the team prepared to dispserse. Annabel was
one of the first away, conscious of the speculation in
Jean's eyes as she looked from her to Drew and back
when he made that appointment. 'Such loads to do. . .'

'Oh, sure,' agreed Jean woodenly.

With more patients discharged than new ones added,
Annabel expected to make up for the time lost to the
ward round. After a rushed but healthful lunch of cheese
and fruit in Physio with Miss Tannoch—who spoiled
her record afterwards by biting absentmindedly into a
chocolate biscuit—Annabel also found time to ring her
mother with the good news about Gran's impending
appointment.

She was naturally very relieved and not at all cast
down at the prospect of Annabel being out that evening.
'Of course I can manage, dear. Nancy is coming round
to use my sewing machine—hers gave out after she fed
it those heavy velvet curtains. Just you concentrate on
having a lovely time.'

Annabel promised she'd be sure to do that and then
hurried back to the wards.

Four o'clock came and went. Only two patients left to
treat now and still no sign of Drew. Jean was taking a
half-day, so Annabel asked her junior, Sister Watson, if
Mr Maitland's whereabouts were known.

'Theatre,' was the brief reply. 'He and Mr Strachan
decided to operate right away on the patient they saw

this morning at the General. They've been at it since two, so they shouldn't be much longer.'

'Thanks, Sister,' said Annabel.

'Any message if I see him before you do?'

'No, thanks—it'll keep.' Just as their date might have to keep, perhaps? But Mr Strachan was on call tonight, so surely he would see the patient through the immediate post-op period. Get your mind back on your own patients, Annabel Kerr!

Last visits of the day for Donnie and the new girl, Lesley. Donnie was definitely hearing now. He wasn't speaking yet, but he had a wide variety of telling facial expressions for all of Annabel's bright remarks.

By contrast, Lesley lay like the Sleeping Beauty, pale and still. 'How is she, Nurse?' breathed an anxious voice behind Annabel as she re-set Lesley's drip after treatment.

Physios were often addressed as Nurse, and they always took it as a compliment. Annabel knew this voice and she said gently, 'Quite as well as can be expected, Mrs Cochrane—and that's not just a formula—she really is.'

'But when will she come out of it, Nurse? It's been four days now.'

'That's really not very long for such a gey big dunt on the head as Lesley had, but the doctors were all quite satisfied with her this morning. . . Oh, look, here's Mr Maitland,' said Annabel gladly when Drew appeared at last. 'I'm sure he can set your mind at rest.'

Drew had, of course, come looking for Annabel, but after a brief smile of greeting he pulled up a chair, sat down with Mrs Cochrane and began to reassure her.

While he was so occupied, Annabel went along to the kitchen to ask the cleaner if there was any chance of a cup of tea for Lesley's mother. 'I sor 'er coming in and

I beat you to it, my duck,' said Mrs McDougall, a
cheerful Sassenach who had met her Scottish husband
while on holiday in Blackpool. 'Comes straight round
from her office every day, she does, and never misses,
bless 'er. I'm just going to raid Sister's bicky tin. . .' She
bustled off.

Annabel then went to the doctors' room to finish
writing up her day's treatment notes while waiting for
Drew. She knew she had plenty of time, because he
never hurried anxious relatives. Hearing him approach
at last, she was ready with a smile. 'You've had quite a
day, haven't you?'

He returned a comical grimace. 'And it's not over yet.
I've still got a home visit to make in Fishertown. A
couple of phone calls and some letters to sign as well. . .'
He looked at his watch. 'It'll be a good hour and a half
before I get back here, I'm afraid.'

If Annabel knew him as well as she thought she did,
he'd likely be even longer than that. 'Alternatively, I
could come with you and take a walk round the harbour—or something.'

'That sounds like a very good idea, just so long as the
something doesn't involve getting picked up by a handsome sailor!'

'If it does, I'll stick a note on your windscreen before
I run off,' she promised.

His sudden grin caused her heart to contract. 'Such
consideration overwhelms me,' he answered, but next
minute he was serious again. 'I'm really sorry about
this, Annabel. But with having to fit in that op——'

'It's all right, Drew. I understand.'

'I hope you always will,' he said, still sounding
serious. But what did he mean? There were several ways
of taking that remark. But Drew had taken her by the
shoulders and was propelling her towards the door. 'Off

you go now and pretty yourself up. But not too much, mind—think of my blood pressure! I'll see you in the car park in twenty minutes.'

'Perfect!'

Today, Annabel was wearing a simple pleated skirt and matching blouse in a soft shell pink, with a wide leather belt which emphasised her slim waist. Over her arm she carried a navy-blue jacket that matched her high-heeled pumps and swinging shoulder-bag. When she came up with Drew, she spread out her skirt and let it fall back into place. 'I hope this will do, but as I didn't know where we were going—where *are* we going, Drew?'

'Can you not wait and see?' he asked teasingly. 'This is almost as bad as taking out an importunate five-year-old!'

'And what would you know about that?' she wondered.

'You'd be surprised. But just to reassure you, you're looking good enough for the Ritz—and well you know it.'

'So that's where we're going, then, is it?'

'I thought of it, but it might have been rather a rush. Unless of course we stayed the night, and I wasn't sure we'd quite reached that stage—yet.'

'How thoughtful you are,' returned Annabel lightly. 'A girl does like to be understood.'

'I've noticed—only some girls are harder to understand than others.'

'And I know a man who's not exactly an open book,' observed Annabel, getting into the Volvo now he had unlocked it.

'Never mind—that's not going to bother us in future, is it?'

'It isn't?'

'No. Did we not agree on Tuesday that it's to be clear signalling from here on?'

'So we did,' she acknowledged, but her answer was drowned by an angry exclamation from Drew as a couple dashed across the road in front of the car, causing him to brake hard. When he had cooled down, he seemed to have forgotten what they'd been talking about, because he said, 'This old boy I'm going to see has some symptoms not unlike your grandmother's, Annabel.' Briefly he laid a hand on hers, folded loosely in her lap. 'Don't worry—if anybody can put her right, George can.'

'I hope so. I hate seeing her the way she is now.'

'I wonder how many girls faced with your problem would have reacted as you did?' he wondered in a thoughtful voice as they rounded the last bend and old Inverdon came into view.

'Coming home, you mean?' Drew nodded. 'Most, I should think. Surely being liberated means freedom to make hard choices as well as easy ones. Anyway, it wasn't a totally unselfish decision. I knew it was nearly time to make a change.'

'Yes—too long in one job on the way to the top is not advisable.'

So he had assumed she meant that career-wise. Annabel didn't enlighten him. Three failed relationships in quick succession got a girl talked about. Nobody had suspected how much she actually longed to fall in love, to marry and have children. But she couldn't, being still too obsessed with the memory of Drew. But now. . .

'Here we are,' announced the man himself as they bumped to a halt outside a tiny whitewashed cottage with an outside stair. They got out of the car and two boys mending nets on the quayside awarded Annabel approving whistles. Drew chuckled and tossed her the car keys. 'You'd better keep these in case you need a refuge.'

The patient's GP had the door open, awaiting Drew's arrival, and when he had gone into the cottage Annabel strolled down the quay towards the harbour mouth.

Fishertown was as old as Inverdon itself; a charming jumble of stone and white-harled cottages, strung out round the harbour, and all leaning cosily together against the cruel east wind. The fishing fleet was now only a fraction of its former size and most of the cottages had gone up-market, becoming holiday houses or the homes of young professionals of the kind brought in droves to the region by North Sea oil.

Drew emerged from the cottage sooner than Annabel had expected, and she hurried to join him, picking her way with some difficulty in her light pumps over the lumpy, cobbled road.

Drew watched her indulgently. 'Why do you not wear the kind of shoes you advocate for your patients?' he teased when she was near enough.

'One, there's nothing the matter with my feet. Two, I'm much too vain.'

'Yes to the first bit—not too sure about the second.' He took an appreciative breath of the tangy, salt-laden air. 'Hungry? You must be after being out in this for more than half an hour.'

'I'm absolutely starving,' she discovered. 'And thanks for not agreeing with me entirely. How was your patient?'

'Very confused. I'm admitting him for investigations, but I suspect those minor absences his GP is so worried about are actually vascular in origin.'

'Tiny strokes due to cerebro-vascular disease?'

'You've got it. And it's such a pity; he's a lovely old boy, Annabel. His cottage is full of mementoes of his life at sea. I bet he could have told a tale or two once upon a time.' Drew took back his keys and unlocked the car. 'It depresses me to see patients I can't help, so I'm relying on you to cheer me.'

'Which of course I shall do to the best of my ability.'

'And who could do more? I'd intended to take you up Deeside to Forbes Castle tonight,' Drew revealed, 'but I guess it's too late now. So Forbes will have to keep.'

'I shall hold you to that. I've heard fabulous reports of that place.'

'You're being very positive tonight, Annabel,' he remarked as they drove off. 'It's most encouraging to a shy, hesitant male like me.'

Annabel threw back her head and released a merry peal of laughter. 'Absolutely incredible!' she gurgled when she'd recovered.

'What is, please?'

'Your estimation of yourself. You're just about the most confident, self-assured man I've ever met.'

'Is that the way you see me?'

'That's the way I see you.'

'Window-dressing. All window-dressing,' he insisted.

'Then you've made a darned good job of it,' Annabel told him. Suddenly aware that they'd driven right round the harbour, she asked, 'Where are we going?'

'In there.' Drew slewed round in his seat to watch her reaction.

'There' was a plain stone building that looked like an old warehouse. 'I—see.'

'No, you don't,' he said, 'but you will.'

They traversed more cobbles and then, on the threshold, Annabel paused and stared. Varnished beams, whitewashed walls, pine tables and chairs, a well-heeled-looking clientele and an all-pervading, totally delicious aroma. 'What on earth. . .?' she began.

'Said to be the best seafood restaurant in Britain—or call it an up-market chippie, if you prefer,' suggested Drew, noting her obvious approval with satisfaction.

'I'm not quarrelling with any of that, if these tantalising smells are anything to go by. And it hasn't taken you long to discover all the best eating places around, has it?' she asked when they had commandeered almost the last free table. Accompanied—or solo? Stop it, Annabel. Don't rock the boat.

'I've got my priorities right *now*,' said Drew with gentle emphasis.

Grey eyes caught and held brown ones. What is he really telling me? she thought. Mustn't take too much for granted. . . 'I'm very glad; that's so important,' she returned simply. The skirmishing was over now and the next stage had begun.

The food was excellent. Annabel knew that much, though she couldn't have told anyone what they'd had. All the time, she was too intent on Drew; what he said, how he looked—and then, while they drank their coffee, the feel of her hand in his. Shall I tell him this reminds me of our little café? she wondered, at the very instant he said, 'I'm remembering our little café. And you called it grotty. How could you?'

'Self-defence,' she admitted, enchanted by this evidence of accord.

After dinner they didn't go back to the car but wandered instead by tacit consent along a narrow wynd that would take them down on to the beach. Here at last, in the friendly half-dark and with only the gently murmuring sea for company, Drew took Annabel in his arms. They clung together, their kisses feverish, embracing ever more fiercely—bound in an increasing frenzy of long-pent need. 'I want you so much,' Drew breathed almost on a groan.

'I know.'

'But not here——'

'The place doesn't matter, just so long as——'

'Oh, my love!'

And then there came a sudden giggling and scuffling behind them in the dark. 'No, Jock, ye cannae. I fergot to put me thingy in!'

'Dinnae gi'e me that. Come here, ye daft quine!'

'Oh, God!' groaned Drew, torn between desire and distaste for the crude scene being played out in the sand-dunes. 'How's that for a turn-off?'

'Never mind—we'll go to your place,' Annabel consoled him between kisses; to be chilled by his sudden brief mirthless laugh. 'What——?'

'Not the best idea you ever had, my darling,' he said almost normally. His composure was returning and he took her arm gently to steer her back towards the light. 'I've waited this long for you—I can wait a bit longer. The setting should be worthy of the occasion.'

'It's—that important to you?'

'How can you even ask that?'

'Oh, Drew!' Just two little words, yet so full of emotion. Her capitulation was complete.

Drew had stopped to take her in his arms again. 'Darling Annabel—so much lost time to make up for!'

'And I can hardly wait to begin!'

'I'm off next weekend,' he murmured against her hair.

'So am I.'

'Could we go away somewhere?'

'It's going to seem such a very long week,' she breathed.

CHAPTER NINE

THE traffic was much heavier than usual as Annabel approached the hospital next morning. Today was Graduation Day, and already the side streets around the University and the Royal Infirmary were filling up with the cars of proud parents, warned in advance of parking problems.

When she tagged on to the tail end of the queue waiting to turn in at the Infirmary gates, there was just one car between her and Drew's silver Volvo. Her pulse quickened and her lips twitched with a tender little smile. Last night had been so wonderful. Misunderstandings were past and the future was bright.

But then the back seat of that Volvo suddenly erupted with an energetic mêlée of children and dogs, so it wasn't Drew's car after all. The driver would be a young mother, then, caught up in the traffic and fretting that she'd not get her bairns to school on time. Annabel glanced quickly at her watch. She was going to be late too at this rate, and she'd been hoping for a precious moment or two with Drew before he started his clinic.

The queue edged forward and stopped again. When it restarted, the Volvo swept in through the hospital gates. One of those high-spirited bairns a patient, then? Surely not!

At last Annabel was through the gates herself—to see that Volvo stationary at the door of DSN, and Drew getting out. The children too. How many? Two, three. . .and all intent on giving him a boisterous, affectionate farewell. Then out of the driver's seat got the stunning brunette who had been with Drew at the theatre. She rescued him from the children and bundled them back in the car, getting her long hair playfully pulled for her pains, before Drew ran laughing into the building.

'Miss? *Miss*?' Annabel came to with a start. 'I thought you must have stalled,' said a harassed porter at the open car window. 'Can you no' see you're causing a hold-up?'

'S-sorry.' With a hand that trembled, Annabel fumbled for the gear lever, bungled the change and sent the car jerking noisily forward. By instinct, she found her usual parking spot, but she couldn't get out. Her limbs were jelly and her stomach heaved. Had she really seen what she thought she had? Thought—that was it! She didn't know; mustn't jump to conclusions.

Take a few deep breaths, unfasten your seat belt and consider. A friendly neighbour, helping out with a lift. In Drew's own car? Try again. The neighbour's car has broken down then, and Drew is lending her his. Better—but on a day when he's on call? She'll be bringing it back later on then. Quite possible. But it didn't explain why those children obviously adored him. Why not? As tots, she and her sister Ellen had adored their next-door neighbour. But then they had lived next door to him all their young lives, whereas Drew had not been back in Inverdon three months yet. Was that long enough to engender an intimacy which also included dating their mother? And taking those children out too. Because he did. 'As bad as taking out an importunate five-year-old,' he had said only last night. And what had he said that very first evening when explaining why he worked in his consulting-room at nights? Because it's so damn noisy at home! Now Annabel felt cold all over. Rowdy children and barking dogs next door could be a problem

in, say, a small modern semi, but Drew lived in Firs
Road, where the houses were large, Victorian and built
of granite.

She didn't want to—heaven knew she didn't!—but
how could Annabel not believe that she had just seen
Drew Maitland saying goodbye to his family? What
other explanation fitted?

No longer cold, but fuming now. All that rubbish
about never having forgotten her! That biggest boy was
six if he was a day. If Drew Maitland had remembered
her for as much as a year it would be a miracle! So what
was he up to? Suffering from the seven-year itch? Then
he could find someone else to assuage it. She'd not be
letting him make a fool of her a second time!

When Miss Tannoch asked Annabel if she was feeling
quite well as she looked so pale and solemn, Annabel
replied that she was dreading what Mr Strachan might
have to tell her later on that day, after he had seen her
grandmother.

'Of course! Forgive me, Annabel—I'd quite forgotten.
Would you like the morning off, dear?'

So kind, but so impractical. Annabel contrived a
smile. 'Thank you, Miss Tannoch, but I'll be better
working. I need something to think about, besides my
own troubles.'

'Whatever you like, dear. The afternoon instead,
then?'

Annabel said yes, thank you, perhaps—if the news
was bad, then she set off for the wards. Now she was
glad to be late. Drew would have paid his early morning
visit and be down in Outpatients by now. The dreaded
moment postponed, and more time to think, which was
desperately needed. Because how the hell was she going
to handle this?

Unlike Miss Tannoch, Jean had remembered, and

after she had given Annabel the usual morning bulletin on their patients she said, 'I suppose your mother'll be bringing her in.'

'Yes. She's going to pretend they're going shopping. Then I'll meet them in the car park and we'll break the news together. That's what,' Annabel swallowed hard, 'Drew Maitland suggested. He said she'd be less likely to protest, once she was actually here.' Why was Jean giving her that funny look?

'This has been a worrying time for you, Annabel— it's no wonder you're looking so wabbit,' said her friend. 'Listen, love. Your grandmother's sure to be admitted, so I'm going to put her in with Mrs Plockton. They'll get on like a barn on fire, I should think.'

'Oh, Jean, that's a wonderful idea. You're a genius!'

Jean grinned. 'It's so lovely to be appreciated—and now here's some advice for you. Try and find time for a coffee break this morning—you'll surely be needing it.'

'Thanks, I will. Now I'd better push off, I s'pose. I'm rather late.' She would try and find out something about Drew's private life some other time. Jean was sure to know.

'Not to worry,' soothed Jean. 'We've only just finished the beds. The clean laundry was late coming up this morning.'

Work. Donnie's first word this morning, and what else would it be but 'bugger' said with feeling, when Annabel wrapped the ice towels around his wasted, contracted limbs? In the gym, Seonaid got to her feet and sat down again several times without grabbing the wall bars. Claire tossed her stick aside and Mrs Plockton wanted to do the same, but was dissuaded in the interests of safety. 'Dear Mrs Plockton,' begged Annabel, 'do remember yours is a different problem altogether. Claire's got one good half——'

'Whereas I'm wobbly all over and more than twice her age and size,' finished the patient, laughing fit to burst.

'I couldn't have put it better myself,' praised Annabel, laughing too, in spite of her inner anguish.

Nurse Kirk was now almost pain-free at last, and shaping up to be another Mrs Plockton in her way. 'Enough is enough,' Annabel had to tell her very firmly. 'Rest now, and we'll run through your exercises again this afternoon.'

Ian Buckie, who had been having a sponge-down earlier, was now being X-rayed so, being temporarily unemployed, Annabel went along to Jean's office.

Jean was on her feet in an instant and over to the coffee tray. 'I'd almost given you up,' she said.

'Sure I'm not interrupting?'

'Oh, come on, Annabel! You know just fine how much I hate this darned paperwork—no matter how necessary. How's things?'

'Fine. Everybody seems to be improving—even Donnie.' She told Jean about his first word and Jean wrote 'uttering single words' in the Kardex, chuckling as she did so. 'Drew will be pleased; he's been very concerned about Donnie.' She hesitated. 'If I have one criticism of that man, it must be that he allows himself to get rather too attached to his patients.'

Which gave Annabel just the lead-in she'd been looking for. 'Yes. What's-her-name—Shona, isn't it?' A name plucked out of nowhere. 'Anyway, she can't see very much of him.' Annabel held her breath.

'Not Shona—Shelagh. And I'm sure you're right. But I gather she's learning to fill her spare time very successfully. She's forced to, poor dear.'

Afraid of showing the shock she was feeling, Annabel turned and gazed out of the window. Drew really did have a wife, then—a wife called Shelagh, whom he neglected. She forced herself to echo casually, 'Poor dear, as you say. It doesn't sound much of a—a life.' The word marriage simply refused to come to her lips.

'I certainly wouldn't want it, but I've never heard Shelagh complain.'

Too besotted, of course. That was the effect Drew had on women, her silly self included. Yet still Annabel couldn't help asking, 'And—and Drew?'

'Drew?' Jean looked at her friend with renewed interest. 'I used to think he was quite happy as long as he was thoroughly overworked. Lately, though, I must say——' She broke off when the telephone began to ring. A moment's listening and then, 'She's right here, Mrs Kerr.' Jean handed the receiver over to Annabel.

'Mother?'

'She'll not come. It didn't work.' Mrs Kerr was obviously near to tears. 'First she said I must be mad to think of going shopping at that time of night. I tried so hard to persuade her, but it wasn't any good.'

'You poor darling! Then how about telling her Dr Faulds wants her to have a check-up? Make it sound like routine for everybody in her age group.'

'Annabel, I've tried all that. She just laughed at me and insisted she's never been fitter in her life. And then—then she had another fit; a big one this time. God, I was terrified she was going to choke!'

'How is she now?' asked Annabel.

'Sleeping like a baby. I rang Nancy and she came round to help me get her upstairs and into her bed. I'm sorry, but it seemed the only thing to do.'

'It certainly was, and I'll explain to Mr Strachan. If I'm not mistaken, he'll probably come and see her at home.'

'The mountain coming to Mahomet,' returned Mrs Kerr with a nervous giggle which ended on a stifled sob.

'Exactly. Now, if Nancy's willing to stay with you, don't you come over all independent and say you can manage—and I'll get home just as soon as I possibly can. Thank heaven I'm off this weekend!'

'Amen to that,' said Mrs Kerr fervently as Annabel put down the phone.

'Gran has gone on strike,' Jean guessed, having heard Annabel's contributions to that conversation.

'Not only that, she's had a grand mal fit as well.'

Jean whistled. 'Has she, by heck? If I were you, I'd make telling that to George Strachan my top priority.'

'Don't you worry—I'll be down there at the double as soon as I've finished my morning's work.'

'Mr Strachan is with a patient and cannot be disturbed,' said bossy Sister Mack who ran the Outpatient Department.

'This is very urgent, Sister,' Annabel told her.

Sister Mack had heard that some relative of the locum physio had been added to an already overflowing clinic list and that, she considered, was quite enough licence granted for one day. 'Then I will take a message, Miss Kerr.'

'It's about Mrs Anderson—my grandmother. She's refused to come to clinic,' explained Annabel reluctantly.

'Mercy me, is that all? There's no need to go bothering a consultant for that. A word to the receptionist is quite sufficient.'

'But, Sister——' Annabel protested uselessly to an already retreating back. Then, her lips set with determination, she stationed herself in the corridor where she had an uninterrupted view of Mr Strachan's door.

Whether Sister liked it or not, she would be delivering her message in person.

After a few minutes, the sight of Drew's tall figure crossing further down the corridor from his room to Bill Tait's brought a flood of mixed reactions. Longing, bitter disappointment, humiliation, anger. . . Annabel thrust clenched fists deep into her tunic pockets. How desperately she had hoped that Jean would look blank and ask what in the world Annabel was blethering about, when she mentioned that girl Shelagh. But Jean had done neither, knowing straight away that Annabel meant Drew's wife. And realising from Jean's reply that Drew's marriage was not of the best was no comfort. He *was* married, and he hadn't told her. Had he been saving up that little detail for pillow talk when he'd got her safely into bed? The rage that washed over Annabel then left her feeling quite limp. But Annabel was fair; she had to admit that, hospitals being the hotbeds of gossip they were, Drew would naturally have thought that she knew he was married—would have thought she was walking into an affair with her eyes wide open. Because an affair was what he'd had in mind all along. God, how is it I'm still so naïve and dewy-eyed at my age and in the anything-goes nineteen-nineties? she was wondering as the door she'd been watching opened, and Mr Strachan's last patient of the morning emerged.

Annabel got to that door in seconds and, slipping in, shut it behind her.

'Ah, Miss Kerr.' Then George Strachan frowned. 'But where is your grandmother?'

'She's refused point-blank to come, sir. And I do apologise, after your goodness in offering to see her.'

'Never mind that, lassie, it's her welfare we're all concerned about. Any new developments?'

'A grand mal fit this morning—after my mother failed to persuade her.'

Mr Strachan looked grave. 'She must be investigated, whether she likes it or not. Give me her GP's name and number and I'll fix up a home visit as a first step.'

Annabel wrote down the required information on the desk pad and passed it to him, just as the door opened to admit Drew. Let me keep calm, please, she prayed.

A bright, intimate glance for Annabel first and then Drew asked his colleague, 'Have you seen Mrs Anderson, George? What's the verdict?'

'She wouldn't come,' said Annabel and Mr Strachan in unison.

Drew shook his head. 'That figures. She's a fiercely independent old lady, your grandmother, is she not, Annabel?' He perched on the corner of the desk, arms folded. 'So what's next, then? A home visit?'

'We'd just decided on that when you came in—I'm just about to ring the GP. Yes, Sister, what is it?' asked the boss with overt impatience when the door was opened and Sister Mack stood in the doorway.

'That extra patient there was all the stramash about has defaulted,' she stated, glaring at Annabel the minute she noticed her.

'Thank you, Sister, we know that and are dealing with the matter.' Pointedly, Mr Strachan picked up the phone.

Sister advanced into the room. 'About the growing size of the clinics, Mr Strachan——'

Annabel slipped quietly out to avoid the row Sister Mack was obviously spoiling for. Poor Mr Strachan, badgered at home and at work, she was thinking when she recognised the purposeful footsteps behind her.

'Er—hello,' she said doubtfully when Drew caught up.

Falling into step beside her, he raised an eyebrow and pursed his lips in a comical grimace. 'Discretion's all very well in this gossip-shop, but do you have to go overboard and act as though you'd seen a ghost?'

'I didn't mean to,' was the best Annabel could come up with.

'How very reassuring! So what about,' he leaned down to whisper, 'lunch?' even though there was nobody within earshot.

'I'd thought I'd just have a—a sandwich. In Physio.'

'Then why are you heading in the opposite direction, towards the canteen?'

'Ah! To buy something, I expect.'

They were crossing the car park now, and regardless of any interested spectators Drew put a sympathetic arm around Annabel's shoulders. 'Poor love! I'm sorry about the teasing—it was very insensitive of me. You're worried sick about Gran, are you not?'

She should have realised he would interpret her gravity that way. So be it—for now. 'Yes, I am. I can—hardly think straight.' How true! 'Supposing Mr Strachan can't persuade her to come into hospital?'

'As a last resort, we could probably have her committed, though I hope it'll not come to that. Does she like your family doctor?'

'Very much. Sometimes she thinks he's her nephew.'

'Then he could be the one to persuade her,' considered Drew bracingly as they reached the staff canteen. Here he freed her, but before he could push open the door one of the consultant orthopaedic surgeons came out. 'Drew—well met. I must talk to you about Colin Montrose.' He ignored Annabel altogether, so, rather than stand there looking superfluous, she muttered goodbye to Drew and went in alone.

That brief encounter had passed off better than it

might have, thanks to his reading of her mood. How kind and thoughtful he had been—not at all like a man planning to cheat on his wife. But then the two were not imcompatible. If they were, then there'd either be many more hard-nosed men around, or fewer unfaithful husbands! As for her own personal disappointment, Annabel supposed she'd learn to handle that the way she'd had to last time. But how was she going to tell Drew that playtime was over, because she knew all about Shelagh and the children? And this time she couldn't run away.

On hearing about Gran's latest crisis, Miss Tannoch renewed her offer of a half-day's holiday. Annabel then asked what about her patients. Miss Tannoch countered with the offer of some help on DSN, as things were quiet in Outpatients. So, thanks to good old British compromise, Annabel was on the road to home by four o'clock. She hadn't seen Drew since they parted outside the canteen, and now she'd not be seeing him until Monday. Would that be long enough to get herself together? Certainly there'd be little time for brooding, with things the way they were at home.

The sitting-room at Rowan House was surprisingly full of people; Nancy, back again after a lunchtime dash round the corner to feed her husband, Agnes, alarmed by reports that young Dr Faulds's car had been seen outside Mrs Anderson's again, and Adam. Nancy and Agnes were easy to greet, but what should she say to Adam after the awkwardness at the Old Mill on Tuesday? 'Hello, Adam—how kind of you to come,' seemed about the safest thing.

'He drove me over—something's amiss with my car,' his mother answered for him, as she all too frequently did. Didn't she realise how diminishing that was?

Annabel turned back to Adam. 'I still think it's very kind of you—and in the middle of your working day too,' she insisted.

'I do have a farm manager,' Adam reminded her heavily. But at the same time, he was also looking slightly less forbidding.

Annabel tried a smile on him before asking, 'Where's Mother?'

'Upstairs lying down,' supplied Nancy before Agnes could.

'I told her she needed to,' supplemented Agnes, regaining lost ground.

'Then I'll go and make some tea,' said Annabel, thinking privately that lying down in the afternoon didn't sound much like her energetic mother.

Mrs Kerr was actually in the kitchen, taking scones out of the oven. 'I'd nothing to give all my kind helpers for their afternoon tea,' she explained with a half-smile. 'Oh, Annabel! Isn't it marvellous? Dr Faulds is bringing your chief neuro-surgeon to see Gran this evening.'

'Mr Strachan will want to admit her for tests,' warned Annabel.

'I gathered that, so I've packed her a case.'

So much for the lie-down Agnes had prescribed. 'And how is Gran now?'

'I keep on looking in, of course, but she's been sleeping for most of the day. Which means she'll probably be bright and clear-headed by the time the doctors come,' added Mrs Kerr with a sigh.

'If she is, Mr Strachan'll not be deceived. Here, let me take that tray through.'

After tea, during which Annabel took over the invalid-checking, Nancy said she thought she might as well go home now that Annabel was there, but wild horses couldn't have dislodged Agnes, who meant to stay and

be in on the consultation if she could. Adam she
dismissed, telling him to come back for her later. For a
moment it looked as if he might defy his mother, then
he gave in with a shrug of resignation.

'He's such a good son,' said Agnes complacently
when Adam had gone. 'He'll make some lucky girl a
gey good husband one of these days.' She looked pointedly at Annabel.

'You could do worse, dear,' considered Mrs Kerr,
following Annabel out to the kitchen. 'Adam's very fond
of you—and I'm sure there'd never be any trouble with
other women.' Poor darling! How she dreaded her
daughters having to endure her humiliations.

'I guess not, but—oh, Mother! Imagine having Agnes
for a mother-in-law!'

That was the first time either of them had considered
that, and they were both smiling at the notion when
Gran came in barefooted, and with her dressing-gown
on back to front. Angrily she asked what a body had to
do to get something to eat in this wretched hotel.

'It can't be ten minutes since you checked,' breathed
Mrs Kerr, snatching off her own shoes and rushing over
to put them on her mother.

Gran fought her off with surprising strength. 'Enough
of that, my good woman. Fetch the manager!' she
demanded in her most autocratic voice.

Gran being now both wide awake and convinced that
it was breakfast-time, they went along with that and
helped her to dress, though not without difficulty. As
demonstrated by the back-to-front dressing-gown, Gran
no longer knew what to do with her clothes, though was
firmly convinced that she did.

When Mr Strachan arrived with Dr Faulds, Gran
was just finishing a bowl of cornflakes. Mr Strachan she
cast immediately in the role of bank manager, and,

turning from him to the bewildered GP, she said sorrow-fully, 'I suppose this means you've been gambling again.'

After a quarter of an hour of bizarre conversation and expert scrutiny—those gimlet eyes missed nothing—Mr Strachan was satisfied. Firmly telling Gran not to worry because he would sort everything out, he ushered GP and family out into the hall, where he addressed himself mainly to Annabel. 'A frontal lobe tumour, if I'm not mistaken, and just what you were beginning to suspect yourself, I'm thinking.'

Annabel nodded. 'Can you——?'

He understood. 'I hope so, but I'll not know for certain until we've done scans and X-rays. Dr Faulds,' he turned to the GP, 'Would you be good enough to keep Mrs Anderson sedated over the weekend? Not too much—just enough for Annabel to get her used to the idea that she's not very well and needs hospital treat-ment. Forty-eight hours should be long enough, so we'll admit her on Sunday evening and get cracking on Monday.'

His calm and positive approach helped Mrs Kerr to come to terms with the probable diagnosis. Gran was seriously ill, but might not be hopelessly so. And she was now about to get the treatment she needed.

When the doctors had gone, Annabel and her mother broke the news to Agnes, who most uncharacteristically burst into tears. But then, as Mrs Kerr said while pouring her a reviving glass of brandy, the two old dears went back a very long way.

CHAPTER TEN

'WHERE am I going?' asked Gran drowsily as they
settled her in the back of Mrs Kerr's car. They were
using hers because it was newer and more comfortable
than Annabel's.

'To the hospital to get rid of those nasty headaches,'
soothed Annabel for the umpteenth time in the past
half-hour. Then she whispered to her mother, 'I'll drive,
then you can sit with her and hold her hand.' All day,
roles had been reversed, with Gran calling her daughter
Mother.

The journey was less fraught than they'd expected, as
Gran was too drowsy to protest much. Not without a
pang, Annabel parked at the main door of DSN, where
Drew's wife had set him down on Friday morning. But
was the pang anxiety for her grandmother, or a knell for
her own blighted hopes?

Drew had phoned her twice that weekend—first to
say how sorry he was not to have seen her again on
Friday, and then to ask how Gran was taking the news
of her coming hospitalisation. Disturbed by his calls,
Annabel was nevertheless glad that each time she had
got to the phone before her mother, or there'd have been
some difficult explaining to do. The second time, he had
had the effrontery to call from home, as proved by the
continual childish laughter in the background. Annabel
had soon terminated that exchange by saying, 'Be with
you in a moment, Adam dear,' to the empty hall. Drew
wasn't the only one with two strings to his bow!

Jean was off duty, so it was Sister Watson who showed

them into the room Gran was to share with Mrs Plockton. It was empty, as Mrs Plockton was away spending the weekend with her daughter. When Bill Tait came to do Gran's admission examination, Mrs Kerr, as next of kin, stayed to give him the details his patient was in no state to provide.

At Bill's suggestion, Annabel strolled along to the doctors' room to wait. She sat down on the low window-sill and gazed absently out towards the main hospital. A trying weekend had been made less so by Adam's frequent yet unobtrusive presence. With Gran about to go into hospital, he seemed to have persuaded himself that Annabel's object with Drew had been to gain his professional assistance. Not being there when Mr Strachan came, he didn't realise that there were two neuro-surgeons and that Gran was not Drew's patient. Annabel hadn't enlightened him. Why bother? Her brief reprise with Drew was over and she was grateful for Adam's concern and support. Now they were almost back to where they had been. Almost. It was Drew who nightly invaded her fevered dreams; Drew whose touch she yearned for. . .

'Annabel, I've missed you!' said the man in her thoughts, materalising just then and sitting down beside her. His white coat, slightly crumpled, smelled faintly of disinfectant, mingling with the masculine smell of him.

Evocative. Too evocative! Annabel would have got to her feet, but for a firm hand on her shoulder and another covering hers. She looked down at that hand. A surgeon's hand, square and strong; well-shaped nails, white-tipped, cut short. A lover's hand that could stroke and thrill. . .but not for her; for Shelagh, his lawful wedded wife.

Annabel stiffened. 'Mr Strachan thinks that Gran has a frontal lobe tumour,' she said in the tight voice she'd not used since her first nervously delivered lecture, years before.

'I know—we've talked.' The hand on her shoulder gently kneaded her taut muscles. 'Poor darling! You're at the end of your tether, but let's hope the strain will soon be over. George is an old hand at dealing with problems like Gran's. Did you know that?'

'I think I—I read that somewhere.'

'Sorry if this sounds corny, but she really couldn't be in better hands.'

'I know.' If only, at this moment, that was also true of me, she thought with regret.

Drew altered his grip to press her against him for a brief moment before getting to his feet. 'What you really need is a brandy, but, as this is a hospital and not a hotel, how about a coffee instead?'

Annabel thought of refusing, but didn't. Weak. . .'You're still busy, then,' she assumed, crossing over to a chair where he couldn't sit beside her this time.

Drew plugged in the electric kettle and spooned instant coffee into two mugs, before turning round to smile at her. 'I have been, but I'm not now.'

'Then you must be expecting another call.'

'No. Knowing your grandmother was being admitted tonight, I guessed you would be here, so I came looking for you as soon as I finished in Casualty.'

'That was—kind. In your place I'd have wanted to hurry home. At the end of a long day. On a Sunday.'

His expression showed genuine surprise. 'Home, for the moment, is simply somewhere to sleep,' he returned matter-of-factly. The kettle boiled and he made the coffee, adding just the right amount of milk to Annabel's before handing it to her. Observant as well as thoughtful. Observant in more ways than one. 'You're in a strange mood tonight, dearest. Are you sure there isn't something else on your mind, besides Gran's condition?'

Annabel waited a moment, knowing what she ought to say, wondering if she had the courage. 'Caught as I am between two attractive men, I suppose mine is a problem many girls would give five years for,' she temporised in a voice of artificial brightness.

Drew gasped sharply. After a tense moment he said tightly, 'I wasn't aware that I was in a queue for your— consideration.'

'You and me both,' she returned quietly. Would he bluster or explain?

What Drew did was to frown in puzzlement. Setting down his coffee with a thud, he crossed the room and towered over her. 'And what is that supposed to mean?'

'One—hears things.' And sees them!

'Now look here, Annabel; just because I've taken Janice Watson out a couple of times——'

Had he indeed! 'Thanks for telling me. I hadn't heard about *her*!'

'Who, then? There's nobody else I can think of.'

So he would never tell her about Shelagh of his own accord. Defeated, she said, 'The fact that you can even think of saying that tells me we're nowhere near the same wavelength after all.'

'If you would only stop talking in riddles, then we might——' he was saying when Bill Tait breezed in with Mrs Kerr at his heels. By now, the whole unit had noticed that the junior consultant was rather interested in the locum physio, and Bill apologised profusely for barging in like that. Mrs Kerr said nothing; just gazed in utter amazement at Drew, before turning to her daughter with a look of deep reproach.

'Mrs Anderson's settled in very well, Annabel, and I've just been explaining to your mother about the tests we'll be carrying out,' said Bill, striving to reduce the tension he could feel, but didn't understand.

Annabel got up and slipped quickly round Drew. 'Thanks, Bill. We're so glad she's here—are we not, Mother? But now we must get back. Anxious friends. . . Goodnight.' She seized her mother's arm and bundled her out into the corridor, heading for the stairs at a swift trot.

Mrs Kerr shook herself free angrily. 'Have you gone mad, Annabel? That was extremely rude. What will that nice young doctor think? And Drew—you never told me *he* was back!'

'Why would I? That was all over and done with years ago.' Annabel hurried on, obliging her mother to follow.

'Are you sure? I saw the way he was looking at you.'

'If you mean what I think you mean, then you're wrong.' Annabel was running down the stairs now. On the half-landing she paused and looked up at her mother. 'Drew Maitland has a wife and three children!'

Mrs Kerr cast a horrified glance back along the corridor and plunged after her daughter. 'My God, what a mess!' she breathed as they reached ground level. Now she was as anxious as Annabel to get away from the hospital. Was she afraid that Drew would come after them?

The phone rang several times that evening, but always the caller was a friend wanting the latest news of Gran. Either Drew had got the message, despite his pretended puzzlement, or he was saving up his indignation for a confrontation in person. The former would be much less traumatic, but, if it had to be a face-to-face, then so be it. It would be very painful, but when had her relationships with men ever been easy? Drew Maitland himself—and could be also her clay-footed father—had a lot to answer for.

'Still gey confused, but not distressed,' said Jean when Annabel asked next morning how Gran was. Jean grinned. 'She didn't reckon much to her breakfast, though, and offered to go down to the kitchen and teach the chef how to make porridge. She seems to think this is some sort of hotel.'

'So much for my efforts to prepare her,' assessed Annabel wryly. 'Would it be wise for me to visit, then, or do you think it might just confuse her further to see me in uniform?'

'There's no telling, but if you want to see her, then it's now or never. A full day of EEG, scanning and so on is planned.'

'Then I'll risk it as soon as you've brought me up to date.'

That didn't take long, there having been no dramatic changes over the weekend, and then Annabel went along to her grandmother's room. Discovering that the old lady didn't recognise her in uniform gave Annabel a considerable jolt. It was so easy to take such things calmly in one's patients, she was thinking as she retreated. And quite impossible to be objective about one's family. Get yourself together, Annabel! You may not be as busy as usual with the weekenders not yet back, but that doesn't mean you've got time to stand about feeling sorry for yourself.

Donnie repeated his first word and several others, less relevant. Odd how the slowly awakening conscious performed. . .Muscle tone definitely down and therefore passive movements easier to carry out. But no sign of active movement yet. Don't be impatient. He's doing as well as anybody could expect.

No change in Lesley Cochrane. At least she hadn't developed the chest infection these patients so often did. It would be such a shame if she had to have a tracheostomy done. The scar it would leave would be so disfiguring, and Lesley was at the most sensitive age. . .

Coming out of the RHI room, Annabel saw the neurosurgeons going into the women's ward. Leave Seonaid until later, then, and take the backs instead; the surgeons would never expect to find her in that ward this early. For surgeons, read one surgeon. By dodging Drew, she was only putting off the evil hour, though he was hardly likely to stage a public scene, was he? I'm an awful coward, decided Annabel despondently.

Nurse Kirk was much improved. 'I'd not be at all surprised,' Annabel felt safe in saying when Nurse asked if she was likely to be discharged at the week's end. 'But you'll need to come for treatment as an outpatient, mind, and there'll be no going back to work for weeks.'

'You're a right wee ray of sunshine, are you not?' returned the patient cheerfully.

Soon afterwards, Annabel overheard Janice Watson telling Bill Tait that Mr Maitland was over in Orthopaedics, checking on Colin Montrose. Breathe more easily, then, and take Seonaid along to the gym. There was almost a disaster when Seonaid, over-keen, tried to stand on one foot and overbalanced. Annabel caught her just in time, but lost her own balance in the process and the pair of them collapsed on to a low plinth.

'What kind of an exercise do you call that, then?' wondered Drew, who had seen it all from the doorway. Having sent Seonaid into giggles and rendered Annabel deep scarlet, he continued, 'If you'd like to come and you have the time, we're just going to do your grandmother's scan.'

'Er—thanks, but I'd not want to get behind with my work,' returned a flustered Annabel, crawling out from underneath the giggling Seonaid.

'You certainly don't appear to be on top of it,' Drew retorted, viewing her discomfiture with obvious satisfaction. 'Still, it's up to you. The offer is there.' He pulled the door to and Annabel thought he was away, but then he looked round it to say, 'There's something I'd like to get straight with you before too long. Do you have any free time today?'

'Not really—except for patients' lunchtime,' she added, suddenly remembering that he would be lecturing to the medical students then.

'How very unfortunate that we can't seem to synchronise,' returned Drew with a look that told Annabel he had seen straight through that.

How very unfortunate that he couldn't also read her thoughts on the important issues. Then again, perhaps not. If Drew Maitland knew how she really felt about him, then she'd be way up the creek without a paddle! 'Come on then, Seonaid. You'll never regain your balance by lying flat on your back, lassie.' Thank heaven for work!

Ian Buckie was surely stronger than at this time last week? Only one way to be sure, though, she must fill in a muscle chart before the round. The weekenders back. Would there be time to treat Claire before lunch?

'I say, Annabel!' called Bill Tait as she passed the open door of the doctors' room. Annabel checked and stepped inside. 'I've just seen a new admission—a PID for operation on Wednesday. He can't remember how long he's had a dropped foot, but thinks about six months, which I find rather strange. So could you get the old box of tricks on to him and test his electrical reactions to settle it? The high heid yins are sure to ask for confirmation.'

'Sure, Bill—no problem. I was just wondering what to do next, now you've decided for me.'

'You're amazing, Annabel. You know that?'

'I always had my suspicions, so thanks for confirming them,' she returned with a plucky attempt at her usual brightness. Claire this afternoon, then—perhaps she'd enjoy the gym with Mrs Plockton and company before the outpatients came.

Mr Hamilton, the new patient, did have a dropped foot all right, but no adaptive shortening of his calf muscles yet. Annabel assembled all the equipment for electrical muscle testing and gently told the patient what was in store for him. 'You'll only feel a funny little tickle,' she promised finally. 'These machines are magic.' Good brisk reactions from the tibialis anterior muscle and in a satisfactory pattern. Nothing like six months, then, but it would seem like that to the poor patient who was having to put up with it. 'It'll take time, of course, but I can promise you that your muscles will gradually strengthen up again, once the pressure on the nerve root is removed.'

'Thanks, Nurse. That's a great relief.'

Annabel was always happy to dish out good news. . . Would Gran be back from having her CAT scan yet?

Five-thirty; a last look at Gran, worn out and sleeping after her hectic day, and Annabel was ready to go off duty. Tomorrow, George Strachan would correlate today's findings and then they would know whether anything could be done. It would be a long evening and a longer night. Would Adam come round again? Annabel hoped so. He didn't say much, but his quiet presence was comforting. Mother was right: no wife of

Adam's need be afraid to look over her shoulder for fear of seeing her successor!

The door of Drew's consulting-room was ajar and when he called out as she passed, Annabel knew he had been waiting for her. Slowly she turned, went in and shut the door. By now, she knew exactly how she was going to handle this with, she hoped, the least possible pain and embarrassment to all.

In two strides Drew was confronting her, arms folded and chin jutting doggedly. 'All right—let's have it,' he said. 'What the hell were you driving at last night? And don't tell me you don't remember, because I'll not believe you!'

'Last night I'd not quite made up my mind. Today I have. I'm going back to Adam.' She'd decided hours ago to say nothing about Shelagh. What was the point?

And she had certainly diverted Drew from his question. He gasped and swallowed visibly, but he kept his temper. After a tense moment he said, 'That's pretty—cool. Are you going to tell me why?'

'I've decided that he's—he's the one for me.'

With a satirical curl of the lip he said, 'Which is why you were so ready to go to bed with me, I suppose. Very logical.'

'That was—very wrong of me.'

'At least we agree about that—or rather we would if I were quite sure I believed you. What has got into you, Annabel?'

She backed away when he looked as if he might take hold of her, because she couldn't risk that. If Drew touched her, her resistance would crumble and the whole mad merry-go-round would start again. 'I was—very mixed up, but you'd better believe I'm seeing clearly now. Like a fool, I was flattered that you should still want me after all this time. But that's all it was, wasn't it? Just wanting. Nothing else; not for me and not for you.' For good measure she threw in, 'I realise now that's all it ever was, only I was too young and inexperienced to know. I'm back on course now, though, and I'm going to marry Adam.' She'd done it now; her boats were well and truly burned. Drew's face was dark with hurt and bewilderment, but Annabel managed to stand her ground, her gaze steady.

She had convinced him. His shoulders slumped and when he spoke his voice was hoarse. 'If you feel like that, then there's no point in continuing this. But I'm very—disappointed in you, Annabel. I thought you were honest and straight and true—not just another cheap flirt, playing off one man against another.'

Couldn't he see that she was equally hurt and out-raged by his deceit and double standards? Angry words for her defence rushed to her lips and died there, because with a final glance of contempt Drew turned his back on her. He picked up the phone and dialled. She was dismissed.

It was with a sense of *déjà vu* that Annabel walked stiffly out of that building. Two farewells to the same man must be something of a record! And it would be difficult to say which one had hurt most. Remembering Drew's long-suffering wife and innocent children, a lot of people would say she'd done the right thing. And doing the right thing was supposed to make one feel good, wasn't it? What a laugh that was!

A woman passing with a crying toddler whose hand was heavily bandaged snatched up her child and broke into a clumsy run as though her child were in further danger from this strange girl standing by her car and laughing aloud at nothing. Annabel didn't notice; just got into the car and drove home.

* * *

Mrs Kerr had been advised not to visit that day, as
Gran would be having such a busy time, and as soon as
she'd asked for and been given the latest news of her
mother, she said, 'Adam is taking us all out to dinner,
Annabel. Is that not kind of him? He thinks that, left to
ourselves, you and I will only mope and worry.'

Annabel surfaced from her gloomy preoccupation
enough to agree with reasonable enthusiasm.

Adam called for them at seven and the drive up
Deeside, beside the winding and turbulent river, might
have been delightful, but for Agnes's non-stop back-seat
driving. Her long-suffering son only answered her back
once. An exhibition of wondrous self-restraint, or just
evidence of hopeless resignation? wondered Annabel, as
with more hindrance than help from his mother Adam
brought them safely to the gates of Forbes Castle. So
this is where Drew meant to bring me on Friday, said
Annabel to herself, as they all got out of the car in the
gravelled car park and surveyed the vast square tower
of pink granite with its tiers of narrow windows, crenel-
lations and tiny pointed turrets. She'd been disappointed then, but now she was very glad they'd not
made it.

The meal was superb, just like the surroundings and
the service. Even Agnes was unable to find any fault.
Adam relaxed visibly in the aura of their concerted
approval. But then he's always more at ease when we're
not alone together, realised Annabel, watching him
covertly from her seat opposite. But then so was she. If
they really did get married, that would have to change,
or life could be difficult. Only they'd not be alone all
that much. Agnes would be there; it was inconceivable
that she would consider moving out. Agnes bossing me
about in the kitchen; Adam awkward and fumbling in

the bedroom! Annabel decided to forget the future and concentrate on the present.

'Yes, please, Adam, I should love strawberries and cream,' she agreed when the dessert trolley appeared at their table.

It wasn't until she got back to DSN after lunch next day that Annabel was called into Jean's office to hear the verdict on Gran. The whole team was there, even Michael, looking awed yet gratified at being included. Over by the window, Drew contrived to be of, but not in the party. After one quick look she'd not been able to resist, Annabel fixed her gaze on George Strachan.

'A frontal lobe tumour, just as we thought,' he began, 'but somewhat larger than I'd expected and not quite in the usual place, which could explain her mild apraxia.'

'And can you remove it?' breathed Annabel anxiously.

'I think we can, though I'm obliged to tell you it'll not be the easiest one we've ever done. I'm being frank, so as not to raise your hopes too much, Miss Kerr. There are always risks, but they must be weighed against the probable benefit and the—er—unfortunate prognosis if we don't operate.'

'I understand, Mr Strachan, and so will my mother. We'll both be in favour.' Yes, Annabel understood all right. Gran might be worse after the operation than she was now, but if she didn't have it she'd get worse and worse and eventually die. On the other hand she could be greatly improved.

'That would seem to settle it, then,' considered the boss. He looked at Drew. 'We'll operate tomorrow.'

Somehow Annabel had forgotten that such a complicated and delicate procedure would require both of them. She snatched another glance at Drew, to find his grey eyes regarding her gravely. 'Do you not think you should tell Miss Kerr exactly what you have in mind?' he asked.

'Your grandmother's is a prime case for Mr Maitland's new technique,' explained the boss calmly, 'so he would be the principal and I would be assisting. However, he seems to think that you might object, though for the life of me I cannot see why.'

While Annabel was still digesting that, Drew said, 'I'm sure Miss Kerr has no wish for her grandmother to be the subject of an experiment.'

There was a short pause and then Annabel said quietly, 'Whatever you decide will be all right by me, Mr Strachan. I have the greatest confidence in your judgement and—and your team.'

'Thank you, my dear. Now would you be interested in seeing the films, etc?'

It was the inside of her grandmother's head he was talking about, and Annabel felt suddenly rather faint. 'If you don't mind, sir. . .'

'I understand—and besides, we ought to be getting down to clinic. Give her some tea or coffee or something, Sister, before she rings her mother, as I'm sure she's very anxious to do.'

As soon as the doctors had gone, Jean set about reinforcing Mr Strachan's decision. 'Operation is absolutely the only course, you know, Annabel dear, and Drew was overreacting when he talked about an experiment. Every one they've done by the new technique has proved its superiority.'

'Yes, I know. I'm not really worried about the—the technicalities—well, not too much. But how in the world are we going to get Gran to sign the consent form? She's been refusing to sign anything for ages. I knew we should have got a power of attorney. . .'

'She signed it this morning.'

'What?' But how——?' gasped Annabel.

'Mrs Plockton, of course. "I was much worse than you, quine," she said, "and look at me now. You'd aye be better to have it done." After that, your granny couldn't get hold of the pen fast enough—and I'd swear she almost understood.'

'Jean, you're wonderful!' Annabel smiled.

'Not me—Mrs Plockton.' Jean poured boiling water into the teapot. 'How's she's shaping up now?'

'Doing very well. She'll never walk without a stick, of course—she'll never be that steady—but she'll be able to get around, dress herself, prepare simple meals, enjoy life——' Annabel broke off, realising what Jean was doing. 'And it's not even discussion time. Thanks for the therapy, Jean.'

'All part of the service,' insisted her friend, 'and do remember Mrs P is also a success story for the Maitland technique. Now drink your tea, ring your mum and then get back to the job. That'll do you more good than anything.'

The afternoon today was almost a repeat of yesterday's, with Mrs Plockton as ever the ringleader. She had worked wonders for Danny's morale—Mr Cairns too. And not only his morale, it transpired! 'Must tell you, quine, he proposed to me over the mince and tatties today. Of course I made a joke of it—I've washed all the men's socks and semmits I'm meaning to this side of Paradise.' She stopped chuckling then and looked contrite. 'I'm right sorry for running on like this when you must be worried sick about your nan.'

'Not half as much as I might be if she didn't have you in the next bed, Mrs P,' Annabel told her.

'Is that a fact, lassie? What a gey kind thing to say! Well, if that's me finished, I'll just away and see if

there's anything she's needing,' and off she went, steering her heavy walking aid between the waiting outpatients in their wheelchairs. Why was it all the
ambulance cases always arrived at once? A girl only had
one pair of hands.

Work all done at last, Annabel went to see Gran.
Passing the day-room on the way, she spotted Mrs
Plockton. She was trying to knit, the needles executing
a lively dance in her shaky hands. She waved her work
at Annabel and called, 'I like to keep busy, quine. Going
to see your nan, are you? That nice young surgeon's
been in with her for a good wee while, so he'll not be
much longer, I'm thinking.'

'Thanks, Mrs P. What's that going to be?'

'A yard o' lace if I dinnae stop dropping stitches,' was
the trilled response.

'And very nice too—I like the colour. Cheerio for
now. See you tomorrow.'

'Aye, that you will,' Mrs Plockton called after her.

Michael would have been chuffed to hear himself
described as a surgeon, Annabel was thinking as she
paused outside the little ward, cheered by the sound of
her grandmother's wicked chuckle. She turned the
handle and went in, halting abruptly in the doorway. It
was Drew, in trousers and shirtsleeves, who was sitting
on Gran's bed and holding her hand. The young
surgeon? But youth was relative and Mrs Plockton was
more than old enough to be his mother. 'I'm
sorry——' she began.

Drew stood up. 'I'm just going,' he said, but Gran
held on tight.

'About time too!' she said to Annabel. 'He's been
waiting ages. And take off those ridiculous clothes—
you're not going dancing looking like that.'

Annabel would have got the picture, even if Drew

hadn't murmured, 'She thinks this is years ago—don't upset her.'

Poor Gran! Never getting her facts right all at the one time. But perhaps, after tomorrow. . . Annabel swallowed hard. 'I'll—I'll go and change in a minute, Gran. Will you be all right while—while I'm out?'

Suddenly Gran's face crumpled. She looked little, pathetic and old. 'I don't know.' With her free hand she plucked at the bedclothes. 'I'm in bed—why am I in bed? It's not dark. Have I got the flu? Have I got the flu, boy?' She knew his face but had forgotten his name.

With his free hand, Drew stroked the troubled brow. 'No, love, but you have got a busy day coming up tomorrow, so you're having an early night.'

'You're a good boy, Adam. I've always said so.' Her eyes flickered over his face again. 'But you're not Adam, you're. . .' she gave up on a sigh. 'I like you better than Adam. And so does she! Oh, go away, the pair of you— I'm tired.'

Drew shook up her pillows as skilfully as any nurse and settled Gran comfortably, while Annabel stood motionless with embarrassment. Then he bent and kissed the papery cheek and taking Annabel by the elbow, steered her firmly out of the room.

'I'm very sorry about that,' she said stiffly.

Drew was putting on his white coat, left lying on an adjacent trolley during the visit. He had thought of everything. 'Why? Your grandmother has a condition of which confusion is the main symptom. Therefore it's only common humanity to play along with it.'

'Yes, I know. What I meant was, I'm sorry for your embarrassment.'

Drew cocked a derisive eyebrow. 'I would say that if anybody is embarrassed, it's you.'

She plunged deeper. 'Yes, but—raking up the past like that. . .'

'Muddling past and present is a common feature of confusion, as you must know.' His voice deepened. 'I appreciate your anxiety, but your grandmother is our patient and I consider that her needs should override our own—lacerated feelings.' And with that, he strode away.

Annabel stared after him. So admirable a man in every way—except the one that mattered most to a woman.

She gave Drew time to disappear, then left the ward herself. She was on duty that evening, so she went to change before going to meet her mother in the Orange Grove for a quick meal. Afterwards, her mother would sit with Gran while Annabel worked; then they would go home together.

There wasn't a lot to do that night. A few immediate post-operative cases who, if left to themselves, might have become chesty and only a couple of chronic bronchitics on the medical side. It would be a different story in the harsh, east-coast winter, though, when the fog rolled in off the sea, bringing respiratory problems with it.

'How is she now?' Annabel asked her mother when, work and visiting done, they met by arrangement in the car park.

'Sleeping. She slept nearly all the time I was with her.' Mrs Kerr frowned. 'She did wake up once and rambled on about you being out dancing. I couldn't make head or tail of that.'

And perhaps that was just as well. Annabel thrust her arm through her mother's and squeezed hard. 'Just wait until she's recovered from that op. She'll be quite different then.' Different? Yes, but better—or worse?

'I don't know how I'm going to live through the next twenty-four hours,' said Mrs Kerr with a catch in her voice.

The first thing that Annabel did next morning was to peep through the observation window of the little ward. Only Mrs Plockton was there, placidly knitting, the ragged yellow piece quite a foot longer than the previous day.

'Your grandmother went down ten minutes ago,' said Jean the instant she saw Annabel. 'She's first on the list.'

'I'm so glad she hasn't got all day to think about it,' returned Annabel, realising as soon as she'd spoken how silly that was, with Gran in her present state.

'Um—quite.' What Jean really thought wasn't for saying. Probably what Annabel herself knew quite well. Trickiest cases first, while the surgeons were at their freshest. Before she could dwell on that, Jean resumed, 'I'm expecting a party of PTS nurses later on this morning for the usual look around, and if you could find time to talk to them about the role of the physiotherapist in neuro-surgery, I'm sure they'd find it very helpful and interesting.' She grinned. 'You could also plug personal back care while you're at it!'

Jean's intention was clear. She didn't mean Annabel to have a minute to brood that morning. 'You don't miss a trick, do you?' Annabel responded admiringly. 'Sure I'll see them. I could slot them in about twelve, if that suits.'

'Perfect.' It was arranged that Jean would bring the visitors to the gym, and then after that they discussed the patients.

And by the look of this, they're also conspiring to keep me busy, thought Annabel, reading over her notes as she went. Ian's muscle chart alone would need an hour. She tried hard to be single-minded that morning, but inevitably her thoughts strayed constantly to that theatre downstairs. Yesterday, the anaesthetist had assured her breezily that Gran had the heart and lungs of a woman twenty years younger. Nevertheless, she was seventy-four. And Mr Strachan had warned that the tumour wasn't the most accessible they'd ever dealt with. But then that was why Drew was operating, using his new technique. . .

The clanging of the lift gates and a rumbling of wheels had Annabel out in the corridor in one bound. It was Gran all right on that trolley the porters were manoeuvring into the little ward. She glanced at her watch; back rather sooner than anticipated. Did that mean that things had gone better than expected, or that it was already too late for useful intervention? Annabel wanted to run and check, but knew she'd only get in the way at this moment. It must be bad enough waiting at times like this when you didn't have a clue about the implications, but when you had. . . Resolutely she returned to the back class she'd been taking. Whatever the outcome, she would hear as soon as somebody had time to tell her.

Jean was smiling broadly when she brought the student nurses to the gym where Annabel awaited them. 'Right, girls. go in and make yourselves at home,' she directed. 'Miss Kerr and I have something to discuss.' She drew Annabel outside. 'Apparently it was all quite straightforward and Drew is said to be quite pleased. He's never more than that, even when he's just dragged somebody back from the jaws, so you can stop worrying, my dear.'

'C-Can I see her?' Annabel asked.

'Sure. Any time you like, but she's quite unconscious and likely to remain so for some time.'

'Yes—of course. I'm not being very professional, am I, Jean?'

'Not particularly, but then you're not exactly heartless, so I wouldn't expect it. Now for goodness' sake go and look at her. I know fine you'll not be easy until you have.'

Gran had been positioned on her side and her head was heavily bandaged. Annabel tried not to visualise what was underneath all that. The shaved head, the neatly removed cap of bone, just as carefully replaced, sutures. . . She must concentrate on the positive. Breathing regular and pulse good. What more could one hope for at this time? Annabel kissed her grandmother's cheek and returned to her visitors.

The next time Annabel went along to that little room, Drew was there, still dressed for Theatre, his brown throat and muscular forearms bare. He straightened up when she entered. 'You've had a report?'

'Yes, thank you. Jean told me things had gone well.'

'The tumour was already the size of a large broad bean, so it's a wonder she wasn't showing more signs. It came out cleanly, though, with minimal insult to the surrounding nerve tissue.'

'Is it. . .?' Was it. . .?'

'Malignant? I doubt it—these tumours seldom are, but we always send a specimen for biopsy. It'll be a while before she recovers from the effects of the surgery, so don't expect too much too soon.' Drew bent a glance on Gran that was almost tender. 'I would expect her to be fully conscious by the weekend. In the meantime, try to be patient.'

'We will. And, Drew—thank you.'

'Not at all. Keeping the relatives informed is all part of the job.'

'I really meant for—for everything.' God, what a stupid word to choose in the circumstances! No wonder he was looking so sceptical. 'I mean—for doing the op yourself. It couldn't have been—very nice. On somebody you know and—and like. . .' What a dreadful mess I'm making of this, she realised forlornly.

'That's all part of the job too. And now I must get back to Theatre. The list is extra long today.'

'Because you slotted in Gran's op,' she realised. 'Oh, Drew, I'm so very grateful.' Why did she feel this compulsion to be so ingratiating?

'I hope we know how to arrange our priorities,' Drew answered stolidly. He went out then, his anti-static rubber boots squeaking on the vinyl floor. Annabel listened to his footsteps receding down the corridor, then visualised him taking the stairs two at a time as he usually did.

Then she looked again at the sleeping figure in the cot bed. No change, and nothing to do but wait patiently as Drew had advised.

CHAPTER ELEVEN

BARBARA CRAIG got a great welcome back, and, not least of all, from Annabel. These last weeks since the collapse of her relationship with Drew had been a tremendous strain—their only bonus being Gran's spectacular recovery. Just this one day to hand over and then Annabel would be back to her original routine. She gave Barbara a quick update on the patients she would remember as they walked across to DSN. 'Colin Montrose is in fine form from the neuro point of view and it's only his fractured tibia that's holding him up— though not for much longer. Claire and Seonaid have both gone home and Seonaid comes to outpatient sessions. She's rather unsteady, so her mother daren't let her wash the dishes, and she's also a trifle excitable and forgetful.'

'Still, when you think how she was when I went off sick,' considered Barbara. 'Now what about Mrs Plockton and Donnie Helm? They both worried me a lot.'

'Donnie's still rather stiff, but he can stand for almost a minute without help now. Mrs Plockton remains a bit unsteady but is definitely improving. She also comes in as an outpatient with Mr Cairns and young Danny. They're quite a trio. I don't think there's anybody else you'll remember.'

'So any minute now, I'm going to find myself as confused as you must have been when you took over from me eight weeks ago,' Barbara summed up wryly as they went to join the party gathering for the weekly ward round.

Not quite, thought Annabel. I had the extra dimension of Drew Maitland to cope with.

She stood quietly aside while Barbara's ward colleagues duplicated the welcome she'd got from the physios. Drew made a particular fuss. As well as being glad to see the back of me, he's thrilled to be getting help with his research at last, diagnosed Annabel.

Mr Strachan was more diplomatic. 'Delighted to see you, Barbara my dear, but you'll be glad to know that your shoes were most adequately and charmingly filled during your absence.'

'I'm quite sure of that, sir. Miss Kerr's treatment manual is the basis for a lot of my work.'

Compliments over, the retinue filed out. As always, they began with the recent head injuries. Drew picked up Lesley's notes first. 'The main problem here is the temporal lobe epilepsy which we're loath to prescribe for as long as we have her under constant supervision and there's hope of spontaneous recovery,' he said, addressing himself mainly to Barbara. 'I'll leave Miss Kerr to tell you about her physical disabilities.'

'Thank you, sir.' Annabel called him sir on every possible occasion, though she couldn't have said why. 'There is moderate impairment of balance and co-ordination with a mild degree of lower limb spasticity. However, I've been working on all of that, and Lesley is walking two lengths of the parallel bars with minimal assistance.'

'And her chest, Miss Kerr?' asked George Strachan. In spite of all their efforts, Lesley had developed quite a severe chest infection, and had needed a tracheostomy after all.

'Quite clear now, sir.'

'Good. Now who else do you remember, Mrs Craig?'

'Donnie Helm, sir.'

'You'll soon see for yourself how much better he is—at least, from your point of view.'

'And otherwise?' Barbara wanted to know.

'He is subject to outbursts of aggression—a combination of neurological damage and frustration, we think. Would you say this is improving at all, Drew?'

Drew looked doubtful. 'Yesterday, in the gym, he threw an Indian club at Miss Kerr.'

Everybody looked at Annabel. 'But he missed me by a mile and he was very sorry afterwards.'

'How do you know that?' asked Bill.

'Because he kissed me.'

Everybody smiled, even Drew, and Mr Strachan chuckled, 'So at least his libido is intact. Let's hope we can eventually restore everything else to the same pitch of efficiency. Now are we ready to go in?'

There were two recent admissions, both still in coma.

'Usual routine, I guess,' whispered Barbara after an expert glance at each. Annabel nodded.

And then they went to see Gran. She sat by the window, working on the *Scotsman* crossword. She looked very smart in a new print dress, and, although her hair was growing again quite well, she clung to the blonde wig she had sent Annabel out to buy for her. Annabel felt sure she always would, as it made her look at least ten years younger.

'Not finished yet, Mrs Anderson?' teased Drew. 'You're usually on to the *Glasgow Herald* by this time.'

'Ah, but this is a particularly beastly one, Drew. Good morning, Mr Strachan. How are you today?'

'Very well, thank you. And you?'

'I feel splendid, so do you not think it's time I went home? You must have people queueing up for my bed, and ours is a big house for my daughter to run single-handed.'

'Funny you should say that,' returned the boss. He turned to Annabel. 'All the latest tests are completely normal, so you may take her home with you today if you like.'

'Thank you very much; I'd better get packed, then,' said Gran, tossing aside her newspaper and standing up. 'And, Annabel, do try to finish earlier than you usually do, dear. I hate being on the roads during the rush hour.'

'I'll do my best, Gran.' Yes, she was cured all right, no doubt about that!

'How did you manage about treatment?' wondered Barbara as they moved on. 'No offence, Annabel, but I can't imagine your grandmother taking kindly to having you for her therapist.'

Annabel chuckled. 'She'd have thrown more than an Indian club at me, I'm thinking! Actually, I got Nessie to come over from Medical Neurology to give her what little she needed. Her problems were mainly frontal lobe, you see.'

They continued thus for the rest of the round, with the surgeons briefing Barbara on pathology and Annabel contributing details of current therapy. When coffee-time came, she would have slipped quietly away, but Jean insisted that she must join them for this last time. There was the usual professional discussion and then Mr Strachan asked, 'What did you eventually decide, Drew?'

'About the flat? I bought it. It's not quite what I was looking for, but it does have the advantage of being only five minutes' walk away from here.'

'As well as being split new. What wouldn't I give for a space-age kitchen like that?' put in Jean half enviously.

'Any time you feel like using it, please feel free,' offered Drew with a grin. 'I can promise you I'll not want to. The Orange Grove will be seeing more of me than ever now.'

Annabel choked on her coffee. Whatever did this mean? She looked from Jean to Drew and back, willing them to expand. But the party was breaking up now and Barbara was waiting for her.

So Annabel was obliged to shelve consideration of the mystery while demonstrating for Barbara the exact techniques she had been using on the trickiest patients. But while she was returning along to Physio at the end of the morning, her mind seized on it again with all the tenacity of a starving Scottish midge.

Split new and only five minutes' walk away? Drew must have bought one of those luxury flats with such a wonderful view over city and sea. Out of sheer nosiness, she and her mother had looked at the show flat one Sunday afternoon after visiting Gran. It was gorgeous; airy, spacious and beautifully appointed, but hardly the most suitable home for a brood of growing children. Wait, though. Hadn't Drew said also that the Orange Grove would be seeing more of him than ever? Did that mean that he and Shelagh were splitting up? If so, bowing out hadn't saved his marriage. She'd done the 'right thing', and still everybody was a loser.

'What news?' asked Miss Tannoch eagerly as soon as she saw Annabel.

Annabel almost blurted out that Mr Maitland was leaving his wife, before realising that Miss Tannoch was actually asking after Gran. 'I'm taking Gran home tonight after work. Isn't that wonderful?'

'Wonderful, but why tonight? Why not this afternoon, dear? That's if Barbara doesn't need you. I didn't know how long the hand-over would take, so I've not got you down for anything specific until tomorrow.'

'Oh, Miss Tannoch, how marvellous! May I really?'

'Of course you may.' Miss Tannoch was always delighted when she managed to please one of her staff.

Naturally Gran raised no objection, so they were on the road for home quite soon after lunch. It was some homecoming. Annabel had phoned her mother, who in turn had alerted Agnes. Agnes had then rounded up all Gran's cronies, and soon the house resembled nothing so much as the parrot-house at the zoo. Having made sure they were well supplied with tea and scones, Annabel escaped to the garden. Down at the bottom under the old rowan tree, she leaned on the moss-covered wall and stared across the fertile strath to the bracken-covered moors. If only Jean had been free when she went to collect Gran! But Jean had been in conference with the senior nursing officer and so Annabel hadn't been able to find out anything more about Drew's move. Yet why so curious? The main fact was surely not in doubt. Drew must be leaving his wife, or else why was he buying a flat? But that didn't stop Annabel turning the matter over and over in her mind all evening.

It seemed strange to be staying in the department next morning, instead of going off to DSN. But Annabel was in no danger of being bored. Miss Tannoch had put together for her as tough a portfolio of outpatients as could be devised. 'Yes, all our problem cases, dear,' she admitted readily when Annabel made a comment. 'Because you're so clever and tactful.'

There's no defence against flattery like that, realised Annabel, becoming aware that the boss was perhaps not quite as vague and disorganised as she appeared.

Miss Wallace, last on the list that Friday afternoon, looked like being the most difficult case of all. A lady of uncertain age and even more uncertain symptoms, she had at one time or another been seen by almost every consultant and certainly every physiotherapist in the hospital. This time, it was Bill Tait who had referred her from DSN with a vague history of neck pain and intermittent weakness in her hands.

But when she walked in, it was her dragging gait that caught Annabel's attention. Under cover of assisting her patient on to the couch, she was able to detect the stiffness in her legs which careful questioning showed to be of very recent onset. Not there when Bill examined her, then. Annabel said nothing to the patient about that, but, having sent her away happy after lots of sympathy, plus some heat and massage for her sore neck, Annabel went over to DSN to look for Bill.

She found him in the doctors' room and confided her suspicions. Bill congratulated her on her powers of observation. 'This puts a whole new complexion on things,' he agreed, 'but fret not, Annabel. Just give me a buzz when she comes in on Monday, and I'll come right over. Are you missing us?'

'Yes and no,' she returned honestly, to which he replied with a laugh that he knew exactly what she meant.

Heaven forbid! she thought, making tracks for Jean's office. Because she couldn't possibly come on to the unit without saying hello to her friend, could she?

But she rather wished she hadn't when she looked in and saw that Jean was not alone.

'Can you not keep away from the place?' asked Drew stonily.

'I had to speak to Bill about one of his outpatients,' returned Annabel, just as distantly.

'Nonsense! You heard the rattle of teacups. Go on, admit it,' laughed Jean, cutting across the chill. 'Come in and shut the door—you're causing a draught.' She was already pouring out a third cup.

Annabel obeyed, but reluctantly. The subject she wanted to raise couldn't be broached while Drew was there.

Jean did her best, but the tea-party was hardly a success and to Annabel, at least, it was a relief when Drew said, surely untruthfully, 'This is all very pleasant, Jean, but I have to go now. I was supposed to meet Shelagh in town five minutes ago. The bossy besom doesn't trust me to choose my own carpets unaided!'

Annabel looked down at the floor to hide her amazement, and when Drew was out of earshot she said carefully, 'So they're separating amicably, then.'

'But of course. Why wouldn't they?'

'Oh—I don't know,' stumbled Annabel, somewhat thrown by her friend's extraordinary attitude. 'I just thought—in her place—I think I'd at least be—well, mildly annoyed.' Mildly annoyed? She'd be absolutely fizzing! That was when she wasn't actually in floods of tears.

'I don't see why. Shelagh always knew it wasn't a permanent arrangement.' Not *permanent*? 'How could it be?'

'You tell me,' returned Annabel, now completely at sea.

'Well, obviously Drew was going to want his own place sooner or later, no matter how close he and Shelagh may be. He must have somewhere to live his own life, as well as a quiet place to work.'

That hadn't clarified things; quite the opposite. 'If you say so,' returned Annabel weakly.

'What do you mean—if I say so? Drew only went to

stay with Shelagh when he got this job because David had reduced her to such a low ebb with his shady deals—and then running off the way he did. And Drew only stayed on because the children are such a handful. But now Shelagh seems to be getting herself together nicely, so he's buying a place of his own at last. How many brothers would have done as much, I wonder? Most men would have been too selfish. Except for the jewels, like my dear old Bob—and Drew himself, of course. Yes, Nurse, what is it?' Jean asked of the girl who had peeped cautiously round the office door.

'Mrs Cochrane was wondering if she might have a word, Sister.'

'Yes, surely. Now don't run off, Annabel. I'll not be a minute.'

Jean needn't have worried; Annabel was in no state to run off. She was too stunned by Jean's revelations. For wife Shelagh, read sister Shelley. Shelley—a wee girl's stumbling attempt at her own name, no doubt; adopted by her family and used until she herself discarded it? Why had she not thought of that interpretation? Dear God, what had she *done*? But there was no time to think now, though, for Jean was already returning. Hide your horror, make a mask of your face. . .

'Her mother wants to take Lesley home for the day on Sunday,' said Jean, bustling in and sitting down at her desk again. 'Must make a note to ask the boss tomorrow, though I did point out that with these little absences she's been having. . .' The note made, she sat back in her chair and looked at Annabel. 'Now where were we?'

Annabel contrived a brief laugh. 'Oh, just gossiping as usual. Jean, Gran wants to do something for the unit, to express her gratitude to you all. Would you have any suggestions?'

'That would depend on how much she's thinking of laying out,' returned Jean practically.

'More than peanuts, by the sound of it. She was quite a time last night trying to decide how much her operation would have cost her without the NHS.'

'Without insurance, and off the top of my head, not less than ten thousand,' supplied Jean, 'which just goes to show how much we need the creaking old battleship. But for mercy's sake don't quote me, in case she sells up to pay up and lands you all in the street!' Jean laughed at her joke. 'Tell you what, you find out how much she has in mind and then I can find out from our consultants what's needed. Talking of whom,' Jean sent Annabel a penetrating glance, 'for a while there, I had the idea that there might be something brewing between you and Drew.'

Annabel swallowed hard. 'Funny you should say that—I kind of half thought so myself.' Yes, that was the line to take. Denials only fuelled suspicions. 'But I think he went off me when—when I refused to help with the research.'

'Could be; his work means just about everything to him. And now, of course, he's got Nessie Drummond involved.'

'*Has* he? I didn't know that.' Was this why Nessie had changed her hairstyle and bought a lot of new clothes? 'But what about Barbara?'

'Alec Craig has put his foot down. He thinks that a full-time job is quite enough.'

'I can understand that.' Annabel rose to her feet. 'I'd better be off now, Jean—I've got a date tonight.'

'The handsome farmer?'

'The very one.'

'Don't get carried away, will you?'

'Not a chance,' returned Annabel, momentarily off

guard, and consequently earning herself a quizzical look from Jean.

The physios were chattering like excited starlings as they changed out of uniform. Friday night euphoria was what the superintendent at St Crispin's used to call it. Well, here's one who isn't exactly over the moon, reflected Annabel, and it's nobody's fault but my own. She took her time about changing, willing them all away, wanting to be alone. If only she weren't going out with Adam tonight!

'You're awful quiet, Annabel,' noticed Nessie. Yes, it would be Nessie! No, I am *not* going down that path again. Look where it got me over Shelagh. . .

'Must be this secret sorrow I have,' returned Annabel with mock pathos. 'You just wouldn't believe!'

That sparked off another burst of laughter, just as she'd intended. Knowing that nobody had an inkling of her true feelings was about the only comfort she had.

But at last they had all left and Annabel could give herself over to some bitter self-criticism. Once, long ago, Drew had dealt her a great hurt. Instead of the hurt healing as she had believed, it had remained there, festering on the edge of consciousness. And so when fate gave her a second chance, she held back fearfully, remembering. She had refused to trust Drew, had condemned him unheard, and now she might never know whether the reawakening had gone as deep with him as it had with her. What a fool!

When Annabel went out to get her car, Drew was parking his. She lingered, so that their paths must cross. 'Er—hello, Drew.'

He checked and looked at her with mild surprise. 'Hello.'

'Did—did your shopping trip go well?'

'My sister seems to think so.' If only he'd called her that before—or had he thought she knew?

'Good. Now I suppose you're going back to work. Or is it research tonight?'

'A bit of both, actually.' A pause. 'You're very interested in my activities all of a sudden.'

'Well, I—I did sort of half promise Mr Strachan that I'd help if he got Gran sorted out, didn't I?' Clutching so pathetically at straws. . .

'I remember, but as I was sure that would be rather distasteful to you I made other arrangements.'

'I see.'

'But thanks for the offer.'

He probably wanted to get on. 'Not at all. Good evening, then,' she whispered, turning away and walking off; not looking back, and missing his thoughtful frown.

Well, what had she expected? She had insulted him and they had quarrelled, and ever since they had settled for a cool and distant courtesy that wasn't likely to crumble the first time she tried to be pleasant. This man was proud.

Annabel shrugged. Then she'd just have to keep on trying, wouldn't she? After all, she'd nothing to lose except her own silly pride, and to play for, there was everything she had ever really wanted. She might even, given the right moment, tell him just why she'd acted the way she had. Though how would she do that? Sorry I was so capricious that time, but I thought you were married and planning to cheat on your wife, and I didn't fancy being a part of it. Charming! And hardly likely to improve things.

It was soon borne in on Annabel that it was one thing to plan a campaign and quite another to carry it out.

The thing might have been relatively simple had she still been attached to DSN. As it was, she could hardly keep running over the road on trumped-up excuses without raising a few eyebrows. Even her friendship with Jean wasn't any excuse, because, now they were no longer working together, Jean made a point of lunching with Annabel several times a week, besides inviting her often to the house.

More weeks passed. Drew's housewarming party came and went, to be described next day over post-lunch coffee by Barbara and Nessie, mostly Nessie.

'I'm rather surprised he didn't ask you, Annabel,' she blundered at one point. 'After all, you were on his unit for a couple of months.'

'If the poor man had asked everybody he'd ever worked with, he'd have had to hire the Royalty Theatre! Anyway, he can't stand the sight of me.' By now, Annabel was past caring what anybody thought.

That's the impression I'd got,' persisted Nessie with prime tactlessness. 'All the same, there are certain— well, social niceties, I s'pose you could call them.'

'Like not opening your mouth and putting your foot in it,' interposed Barbara, turning her back on Nessie and changing the subject. 'I'm awfully sorry, Annabel, but there's going to be an awful lot to do on my unit this weekend. I hope you don't mind.'

'Not in the least. If I've got to be here, I much prefer to be busy.' Once, Annabel would have been delighted to have a lot to do in DSN on a weekend that coincided with Drew's. Not any more. Not being invited to his party had proved how his interest in her had waned. It had cut her to the quick and caused her to give up hope. 'Has anybody got a copy of this month's journal?' she asked. 'I seem to have left mine at home.'

Several were offered, and Annabel reached out for the nearest one, then retired to a quiet corner seat to read.

When she came across the advertisement, she read it twice with care; then thought carefully. Gran was now better than she'd been for years. As for the future, Edinburgh was less than three hours' drive away. She missed her teaching, and senior lectureships didn't come up all that often. Now that she'd been awarded her Fellowship her qualifications were surely adequate. There was no harm in applying. She would talk it over with Jean tonight.

By mid-afternoon, it was clear that this was going to be a real humdinger of a weekend, with acute chests on almost every unit. 'And with all that travelling as well. . .' Miss Tannoch shook her head of wiry grey hair. 'You'll need to sleep in, Annabel.'

'It's all right, Miss Tannoch. I'm weekending with Sister Fyvie. Her husband's away on a course, so I'll be company for her, as well as being on the spot.'

But not much company tonight, thought Annabel, recalling that conversation as she parked in the Fyvies' drive well after ten. Jean came to the door in her dressing-gown. 'You puir wee soul!' she exclaimed. 'What would you like first? A drink and something to eat, or a nice long soak in the tub?'

Not having eaten since lunchtime, Annabel opted for food. After she had demolished the outsize open sandwich Jean fetched for her, she broached the subject of the lectureship in Edinburgh.

Jean poured more coffee for them both while she thought about it. 'This is rather unexpected, Annabel,' she said at last. 'I know you miss your teaching, but what about Adam?'

'Adam?' Annabel hadn't even considered him in this. 'We seem to be—sort of stuck at the moment.'

'And are you hoping that if you distance yourself, but not too much, it might give him the necessary jolt?'

Annabel hadn't expected Jean to think along those lines. 'Not really. Adam's a dear, kind, good man, but somehow—' she paused, seeking the right words, 'I can't really see our relationship going anywhere and I'm pretty sure he's got his doubts too.'

'In that case, I definitely think you should go ahead.' A tiny smile. 'And I for one will be very interested to see what happens. Have some fruit?'

'No, thanks, I've had plenty to eat.' But what had Jean meant about being very interested in the outcome? 'Are you thinking that I may not get it, then?'

'The job? Of course you will, with your reputation. But your departure could cause a few ripples.'

'Ah, now I see what you're getting at. I've not been long at the Royal, have I? But surely that'll not be held against me, now that the reason for giving up teaching and coming home no longer exists.'

Jean's laugh held a mixture of fondness and exasperation. 'For a girl of your undoubted intelligence, you can be remarkably obtuse, young Annabel! But go after that job by all means. It, or something like it, is exactly what's needed.'

'You really think so?'

'I'm certain of it.'

'Thanks, Jean, then I will.' Annabel wrinkled her nose. 'I shan't half miss you, though.'

'That's the way it goes, quine. And now, after all that good advice, the head girl prescribes a nice relaxing bath!'

Saturday was reasonable, with four physios on duty in the morning, but Sunday promised to be a day to remember. Annabel made a very early start, beginning with the surgical wards.

'One theatre closed due to staff problems; that's why there were so many major ops on Friday,' explained a harassed sister. 'You'll be coming back to my hemi-colectomy every two hours, I hope. I'm not wanting him to burst his stitches coughing unaided.'

'I'll do my very best, Sister,' was the most Annabel could promise, with all those chronic bronchitics pant-ing away on Medical and three recent head injuries brewing up chest infections. So which way next, then? Better make it DSN. DSN was the nearest, and jogging there would save more precious minutes.

Jean seconded a nurse to do the suction, while Annabel performed the ritual percussion, which was a great time-saver. Usually the physio had to do both. Nevertheless, when Jean intercepted her to offer coffee as she sped past the office, Annabel refused.

'Are you quite sure, Annabel? Having Nurse's help must have saved you a good fifteen minutes, and sometimes a little break works wonders.'

'I'll be lucky if I even get lunch today,' Annabel confided ruefully.

'Good heavens—I'd better stand by with an outsize supper, then,' reckoned Jean.

Annabel thanked her and hurried on. Coffee would have been very welcome, but not with Drew there. What a good thing she'd heard his voice, like that. Jean was a darling, but not too perceptive.

It was ten p.m. before Annabel plodded wearily up the stairs to the surgical neurology wards for the fourth and, she hoped, the last time that day. She couldn't remem-ber ever feeling quite so weary; her fatigue due as much to the ceaseless fight against the clock as to all the physical energy expended. And there'd been no time for those little chats after therapy which meant so much to the patients; making them feel that you were interested in them as people, and not just in their ailments. But now, just three more treatments and then she could drive to Jean's and climb thankfully into a comforting hot bath. . .

Drew was coming out of the RHI room. His white coat was thrown over his shoulder and he was rolling down his shirtsleeves. 'I had to change Jim Duncan's tracheostomy tube,' he said. 'I gave him a good clean out while I was at it, so that's one less for you.'

'Thanks, but he's got a lot of basal secretions, so perhaps I'd better——'

'He may have had earlier, but he hasn't now. You must have cleared them at the last treatment.' He regarded her narrowly, not missing the weary droop of her shoulders and the dark smudges under her lustreless brown eyes. 'You look all in. Have you got much more to do?'

'Only Charlie and Hamish, if Jim is clear.'

'You'll be glad to be finished,' he assumed, giving her the first smile he'd spared her in weeks, before walking on.

Annabel went into the little room. How many chests had she percussed that day? Thirty? Thirty-five? No wonder her arms were aching. . .

At last she was leaving. Drew's consulting-room door was ajar and there was the subdued glow of lamplight within. Working again? Did he never rest?

He appeared in the doorway. 'Annabel?' She halted. 'Come in, please.'

Slowly she complied. He'd hardly spoken to her for weeks. What a time to choose!

He didn't ask her to sit down, but closed the door

before striding over to the inevitable coffee-maker. He poured some into a mug and handed it to her without speaking.

She took it and said, 'This is very kind of you.'

Drew shrugged. 'It'll keep you going until you get to Jean's.'

'Yes.' Pause. 'Jean is a very good friend to me.'

'You'll miss her when you go to work in Edinburgh.' He folded his arms across his broad chest and regarded her earnestly. 'And that's something which puzzles me. It's not three months since you told me you were getting married. How are you going to reconcile the two?'

'I'm—not,' she returned jerkily.

'No?' Drew looked down at the floor for a second, then fixed her with a probing look. 'You're moving to another farm further south, perhaps.'

'No. Adam and I are not getting married. It would never have worked, because I'm—I'm not in love with him.'

There was a noticeable relaxation in his stance as Drew observed thoughtfully. 'It seems to me that you're rather good at *not* being in love, Annabel.'

'Correction. What I am is very *bad* at being *in* love. It—it frightens me,' she admitted on a whisper.

Without conscious volition, they had been drawing closer and Drew was quite near as he responded, 'I can understand that.'

'You can?' she breathed, staring up at him, her eyes wide with amazement. 'But—you're always so sure. . .'

Diffidently he said, 'Being sure doesn't always mean being right.' He paused, seeking the right words. 'That's something I discovered eight years ago, when I made a terrible mistake which I've been regretting ever since— and didn't make much of a job of trying to rectify.'

What else *could* he mean but. . .? Annabel laid a

tentative hand on his sleeve. 'If you mean what I—I hope you mean, then it wasn't your fault. You didn't get any help.'

'No, I didn't, did I?' he agreed. 'Quite the reverse, in fact. A snub like that was enough to put a man off for life.'

He was so close now that Annabel could feel his warm breath on her cheek. Her hand travelled upwards of its own accord to cup his shoulder. 'I wish I knew how to—to put things right,' she whispered.

'And I wish I could be sure you really want to,' Drew whispered back. 'But all this blowing hot and cold. . .'

'Oh, Drew that was only because I didn't know where I was—and now I'm so ashamed, so sorry. Can you ever forgive me?'

'I'm willing to give it a try,' he responded exultantly, gathering her close for a long kiss that left them both breathless.

'Marry me soon, Annabel,' he urged some time later, against her quivering mouth.

'Oh, Drew—yes, please!'

'And I mean very soon—before you change your mind again.'

'But I'll not do that—not ever, my darling.'

Drew stretched out a hand and pretended to switch on the desk-top recorder. 'Would you mind repeating that? I'll feel much safer if I've got it on tape.'

Annabel giggled. 'Drew, you are an idiot—no wonder I've always adored you!' Her heart put in an extra beat at the fire in his eyes as she said that.

'Just as I have adored you, my precious little love. What almighty fools we've been,' he groaned as he folded her close again. Lovely moments then. Happy moments, revelling in the feel of each other, kisses, murmured words of love, promises, faith in their future. . . And then just when Annabel was feeling that nothing could ever go wrong between them again, Drew asked, 'Darling, what did you mean when you said you didn't know where you were?'

'Please forget that, darling. I was just—being silly, that's all.' She kissed him lingeringly, but Drew meant to have an answer.

'How could you possibly have been in doubt after that night when we went to Fishertown?' Now he was frowning. 'And yet later—you said some pretty hurtful things, Annabel. There had to be a reason for that.'

She winced at the memory, knew she owed him an explanation—and dreaded his reaction. 'Darling— please, please try not to be cross.'

'I promise.'

'Or—or take it all back?'

'Surely that's not very likely?'

'I—I saw you with Shelagh and her children.'

He raised his eyebrows in comical astonishment. 'So?'

'I thought—I thought that she was—your wife!'

'My——?' He released her as though she was suddenly too hot to handle. 'Good heavens, Annabel, if I had a wife and all those children, what the hell was I doing dangling after you?'

'J-Just what I wondered.'

'Thanks for the vote of confidence!'

'I knew you'd be cross,' she moaned.

'Cross? I'm not cross—I'm bloody furious! I've a damn good mind to put you across my knee!'

'And nobody could blame you,' she agreed meekly, her eyes huge with contrition. 'I certainly deserve it.'

They stared at each other for a tense moment more and then Drew's face slowly relaxed in a smile as he said, 'Except that spanking is not exactly what I'm aching to do to you.' He pulled her close again.

'And I can think of—of a much better way to show you how sorry I am.'

He traced the outline of her soft mouth with a thoughtful finger. 'You've not seen our new home yet, have you?'

'No—and I'm just dying to.' Her weariness was all forgotten now.

'Then what are we waiting for?' he asked softly, kissing her once more—just to be going on with.

A ROMANTIC TREAT FOR YOU AND YOUR FRIENDS THIS CHRISTMAS

Four exciting new romances, first time in paperback, by some of your favourite authors – delightfully presented as a special gift for Christmas.

THE COLOUR OF DESIRE
Emma Darcy

CONSENTING ADULTS
Sandra Marton

INTIMATE DECEPTION
Kay Thorpe

DESERT HOSTAGE
Sara Wood

For only £5.80 treat yourself to four heartwarming stories.

Look out for the special pack from 12th October, 1990.

4 MEDICAL ROMANCES
AND 2 FREE GIFTS
From Mills & Boon

Capture all the excitement, intrigue and emotion of the busy medical world by accepting four FREE Medical Romances, plus a FREE cuddly teddy and special mystery gift. Then if you choose, go on to enjoy 6 more exciting Medical Romances every two months! Send the coupon below at once to:

**MILLS & BOON READER SERVICE, FREEPOST
PO BOX 236, CROYDON, SURREY CR9 9EL.**
No stamp required

✂ — — — — — — — — — — — — — — ✂

YES! Please rush me my 4 Free Medical Romances and 2 Free Gifts! Please also reserve me a Reader Service Subscription. If I decide to subscribe, I can look forward to receiving 6 Medical Romances every two months for just £8.10 delivered direct to my door. Post and packing is free, and there's a free Mills & Boon Newsletter. If I choose not to subscribe I shall write to you within 10 days – I can keep the books and gifts whatever I decide. I can cancel or suspend my subscription at any time. I am over 18.

EP89D

Name (Mr/Mrs/Ms) _____

Address _____

_____

_____ Postcode _____

Signature _____

A Free Mills & Boon Romance for you!

t Mills & Boon we always do our best to ensure that our books are
st just what you want to read. To do this we need your help! Please
pare a few minutes to answer the questions below and overleaf
nd, as a special thank you, we will send you a FREE Mills & Boon
Romance when you return your completed questionnaire.

We'd like to find out about your holiday habits and holiday
reading, so that we can continue to provide you with the high
quality Romances you have come to expect.

**Don't forget to fill in your name and address so we know
where to send your FREE BOOK.**

Please tick the appropriate boxes to indicate your answers. ☑

1 **How many hoildays do you have a year?**

None ❑   1 ❑   2 ❑   3 ❑   More than 3 ❑

2 **Have you been on holiday**   Yes ❑
within the last year?   No ❑

3 **If YES where did you go?**_____

4 **When taking holidays do you normally go?** (tick only one)

(a) Europe ❑   (b) U.K. ❑
(c) Outside Europe ❑   (d) Other_____

Please complete overleaf

5 **How do you usually travel to your holiday destination?**
(tick only one)

(a) Coach ☐   (b) Train ☐   (c) Plane ☐
(d) Boat ☐   (e) Car ☐

6 **What type of holiday do you usually have while you are away?**

(a) Coach ☐   (b) Caravan ☐   (c) Hotel ☐
(d) Holiday Camp ☐   (e) Bed and Breakfast ☐   (f) Villa ☐

(g) Other_____

7 **Do you usually take a Mills & Boon Romance with you?**   Yes ☐   No ☐

(a) If YES, How many?   1 ☐   2-4 ☐   4+ ☐
(b) If NO - Do you take any other books?   Yes ☐   No ☐

Type of book e.g. mystery, biography.

_____

8 **Do you buy books while you are away?**   Yes ☐   No ☐

9 **Which age group are you in?**

Under 25 ☐   25-34 ☐
35-54 ☐   55-65 ☐

Over 65 please state_____

10 **Are you a Reader Service subscriber**

Yes ☐   No ☐

If YES Sub No.

_____

Thank you for your help. We hope that you enjoy your FREE book.

Post this page TODAY TO: Mills & Boon Reader Survey FREEPOST P.O. Box 236, Croydon CR9 9EL. (No stamp required)

Mrs/Ms/Miss/Mr_____ EDC

Address_____

_____

_____

_____ Postcode_____